"You're cold." He shoved his gun in the holster and started to unstrap his Kevlar vest as if to wrap it around her.

She placed her hand on his, stopping him. "No. That's all you have to keep yourself warm. You already gave up your shirt for me. I'll not have you freeze to death by giving me your vest."

He nodded. "At least this cave is dry. I'd start a fire but it would be a beacon to the gunmen. Come on. Sit and we'll huddle together to get warm."

The images *that* conjured in her mind had her feeling warm all over.

"I promise I'll behave," he added, as if he thought she might be worried about his intentions.

Ashley snorted. "Don't expect me to make the same promise."

He chuckled and pulled her closer. "Are you always this shy, or am I special for some reason?"

Oh, he was definitely special, but no way was she saying *that*.

TENNESSEE TAKEDOWN

LENA DIAZ

Thank you, Allison Lyons and Nalini Akolekar.

Recycling programs for this product may not exist in your area.

This one is for Sean and Jennifer, and the fun memories of horseback riding and white-water rafting in Tennessee. Exploring the Smoky Mountains with you was a true joy. Looking forward to many more years of happy memories to look back on. Am so *very* proud of both of you. Love you.

ISBN-13: 978-0-373-69743-4

TENNESSEE TAKEDOWN

This edition published by arrangement with Harlequin Books S.A.

For questions and comments about the quality of this book, please contact us at CustomerService@Harlequin.com.

Printed in U.S.A.

ABOUT THE AUTHOR

Lena Diaz was born in Kentucky and has also lived in California, Louisiana and Florida, where she now resides with her husband and two children. Before becoming a romantic suspense author, she was a computer programmer. A former Romance Writers of America Golden Heart® finalist, she has won a prestigious Daphne du Maurier award for excellence in mystery and suspense. She loves to watch action movies, garden and hike in the beautiful Tennessee Smoky Mountains. To get the latest news about Lena, please visit her website, www.lenadiaz.com.

Books by Lena Diaz

HARLEQUIN INTRIGUE

1405—THE MARSHAL'S WITNESS
1422—EXPLOSIVE ATTRACTION
1466—UNDERCOVER TWIN
1476—TENNESSEE TAKEDOWN

CAST OF CHARACTERS

Dillon Gray—Horse farm owner in the Smoky Mountains town of Destiny, Tennessee, he's also a detective and leader of the SWAT team. When a killer targets Ashley Parrish, Dillon must keep her safe while figuring out who wants her dead.

Ashley Parrish—This self-employed businesswoman is in Destiny on a temporary assignment when she's almost killed in a workplace shooting. But that's only the beginning of her troubles when she turns to sexy Detective Dillon Gray for protection.

Ron Gibson—Owner of Gibson & Gibson Financial Services. His son is one of the casualties in the workplace shooting. Does he blame Ashley for his son's death?

Chris Downing—Detective and SWAT officer, he grew up always being second best to Dillon. Is he Dillon's best friend, or does he resent him and have a secret agenda?

Lauren Wilkes—Ashley's best friend since high school, Lauren is on a cruise when Ashley is almost killed. Her call to the police saves Ashley's life.

Chief Thornton—Police chief of Destiny, Tennessee, P.D. He resents Dillon's habit of undermining his authority.

Donna Waters—Only female police officer in Destiny; SWAT team member; best shooter on the force.

Todd Dunlap—The shooter at Gibson & Gibson. Was he alone, or is someone behind his actions?

Iceman—This killer relentlessly pursues Ashley when the workplace shooting fails.

Jason Kent—FBI agent who sends the investigation in a totally new direction, making everyone question everything.

Chapter One

Ashley edged farther under the desktop in the cubicle, her fingers clutching the phone to her ear, her knees scraping against the coarse commercial carpet. *Breathe...in, out, in, out. Focus, listen. Where is he?*

Her breaths wheezed between her teeth, making a sharp whistling sound.

Calm down. He'll hear you if you don't calm down.

"Why don't I hear any sirens yet?" she whispered to the nine-one-one operator.

"They're on the way, ma'am. Is the shooter still in the building?"

"I'm not sure. I think so."

"Stay where you are. Stay on the line. The police will be there soon."

Her fingers tightened around the phone. That's the same thing the operator had told her *ten minutes ago*—after the shooter killed Stanley Gibson.

They'd both been standing by the copier, chatting about nothing in particular while the machine spit out reports for their next meeting. A soft *pfft* sound whooshed through the air. A bright red circle bloomed on Stanley's forehead. His eyes rolled up and he crumpled to the floor.

Ashley had stood frozen, too horrified to acknowledge what her subconscious already knew—someone had just shot one of her coworkers.

That's when the screams began.

She'd whirled around. The shooter stood in the main aisle, his silver hair forming spikes across his head like porcupine quills. His dark gaze locked on her.

And then he smiled.

Ashley's fight-or-flight instincts had kicked in. She ran. Around the corner, past the glass-enclosed offices the managers used. *Empty. Thank God.* At least half the company was out to lunch. But the rest were here, like her, trapped between the shooter and the only exit.

She kept running, to the other side of the building, to another maze of cubicles. She dove into the nearest one and grabbed the phone from the top of the desk. That was when she'd called nine-one-one.

A terrified scream echoed through the room.

Ashley's pulse sputtered. "He's still here," she whispered.

"Help is on the way."

The operator's calm, matter-of-fact tone had Ashley clenching her teeth so hard her jaw ached. Didn't the operator realize people were dying? Had the woman even *called* the police?

Leaning as far out of the cubicle as she dared, she risked a glance down the main aisle. The shooter's progress through the offices of Gibson and Gibson Financial Services was marked by screams and shouts coming from the other side of the building.

The mournful wail of police sirens erupted outside the windows.

Thank you, thank you, thank you!

"I hear sirens," she whispered. "They're close."

"Yes, ma'am. Are you still in the same location?"

"I haven't moved."

"I've notified the police where you are. They'll be there soon."

Ashley was really starting to hate the word *soon.* And she also sorely regretted taking the auditing contract in Destiny, Tennessee. If she were in her home office in Nashville right now, she wouldn't be cowering in a cubicle with a crazed shooter on the loose.

One of the young temps stuck her head out of another cubicle several aisles away. What was her name? Karen? Kristen? Ashley had only met her once and couldn't remember. The girl's face was ghostly pale, her eyes wide with terror as she silently begged Ashley for help.

Ashley's stomach jumped as if she'd plunged down a steep drop on a roller coaster. The girl couldn't be more than nineteen. Ashley *had* to help her. But how? Which cubicle was safer? Should she run to the girl, or have the girl run to her?

She sucked in a breath. *Oh, no.* Spiky gray hair showed above a row of cubicles down a side aisle. *The shooter.* And he was heading straight toward the temp.

Ashley frantically motioned for the girl to hide.

The girl's brow furrowed and she raised her hands in the air, not understanding what Ashley was trying to tell her.

In a few more steps, the gunman would be able to see them both.

"Go back," Ashley mouthed, desperately pointing at the approaching shooter.

He rounded the corner. Ashley ducked back behind the partitioned wall.

A high-pitched scream echoed through the room, then abruptly stopped.

She clamped her hand over her mouth. *No, no, no.*

A shoe scraped across the carpet. Ashley froze. A swishing sound whispered through the air, as if someone had brushed up against one of the fabric-covered cubicle walls. Close.

Too close.

"Ma'am, the police are evaluating the situation," the operator said through the phone in her monotone voice.

Ashley quickly covered the receiver. Her pulse slammed in her ears as she waited, listened. Was the shooter the one who'd made that swishing noise? Had he heard the operator? Her hand shook as she gingerly hung up the phone. She couldn't wait for the police anymore. If she didn't do something, right now, she'd be as dead as Stanley Gibson.

DILLON GRAY CROUCHED beneath the window, cradling his assault rifle. He and the rest of his six-man SWAT team waited for the green light to begin the rescue operation in the one-story office building of Gibson and Gibson Financial Services.

Beside him, his friend since childhood, Chris Downing, watched the screen on his wristband, showing surveillance from the tiny scope he'd raised up to the window. "Casualties at three and five o'clock," he whispered into the tiny mic attached to his helmet. "One more at eleven o'clock. No sign of a shooter."

Dillon's earpiece crackled and his boss's voice came on the line. "Witnesses indicate there could be two shooters. Descriptions inconsistent. Shooters are dressed in black body armor. Kill shot will be a headshot. They're using handguns. No long guns or explosives reported."

"Do we have the go ahead to move in?" Dillon asked, inching closer to the door.

"Negative. Still gathering intel. Hold your position."

His team looked to him for direction, their faces taut with frustration. They wanted to go in as badly as he did.

"Do we have a count yet on how many civilians are inside?" Dillon asked his boss.

"Negative," Thornton replied. "Workers are still pulling into the parking lot after lunch. Impossible to know how many escaped and how many remain."

Meaning there could be dozens or more inside. Defenseless. Hiding under desks, in conference rooms, in closets, waiting, praying someone would help them. What chance did an unarmed office worker have against men with guns, picking them off like targets at a gun range?

The stock of his rifle dug into Dillon's clenched fist. The Destiny, Tennessee, police department was small and more accustomed to patrolling acres of farmland and gravel roads than suiting up in flak jackets and storming buildings. His SWAT team consisted of beat cops, desk jockeys and other detectives like him, but they'd all been hunting and shooting since they could walk. And they trained regularly, and hard, for this type of situation. What was the point of that training if they cowered and did nothing? How many civilians had died in the few minutes his team had been crouching beneath the windows? How many of those civilians were their own friends and neighbors?

"The team is ready and willing to go. *Strongly* requesting permission to enter, sir."

"Negative," Thornton replied. "Stand down, Detective Gray. Await further instructions."

Dillon cursed.

Chris tapped his shoulder. “Movement on the east corner,” he whispered. “Appears to be a civilian. Belly crawling toward the exit.” His tortured gaze shot to Dillon. “Heavy blood trail.”

Dillon closed his fist around the mic so his boss wouldn’t hear him as he addressed his team.

“Chief Thornton ordered us to sit tight and wait. You’ve got nothing to be ashamed of if you follow orders. Some of you have families to support. I don’t. If he fires me, so be it. But I’m not waiting one more minute while people die inside. I’m going in.”

Every one of his teammates raised their thumbs, letting him know they were all in.

He glanced at the only woman on the team, Donna Waters.

“Don’t even say it,” she warned. “You’ve never been sexist before. Don’t start now. I’m not waiting outside while the guys get all the fun.”

Dillon ruefully shook his head and held his fingers in the air. “We go in five, four—”

“Gray, what are you doing?” Thornton demanded. “I told you to stand down. That’s an *order.*”

“—one.” Dillon waved his hand in a forward rolling motion.

Donna yanked the door open. Dillon ran inside, first as always, crouching down, swinging his rifle left to right, covering his team as they rushed in behind him.

“Clear,” Dillon whispered, thankful his boss had shut up, leaving the airway free for communication among the team. When this was over, Thornton would give him hell, or fire him. But for now, the chief knew to butt out.

Dillon pointed to the injured civilian trying to crawl to the door. The two closest men grabbed the injured man and carried him outside. Dillon gave Donna a signal to wait for the two men to return before beginning her search on the west side of the building, while he and the two men with him headed to the east side.

The building formed a rectangle, with rows of six-foot-high cubicle walls divided in the middle by a line of glassed-in offices, bathrooms and conference rooms. Solid walls acted as firebreaks every twenty feet. The two teams would have to search and clear each section in a grid pattern before moving to the next.

When he reached the first body, Dillon sucked in a quick breath. The man was only a casual acquaintance, but Dillon had shared math classes with him in high school. The shooter, or shooters, had gone for a head shot. The vic never had a chance.

They continued on, finding two more casualties. A scratching sound whispered from the next aisle. Dillon crouched down and signaled his men to approach in a flanking maneuver from each end of the aisle. When they were in position, he held up five fingers, counting down. *Four. Three.* He rushed into the cubicle in front of him, silently continuing the countdown, as he knew his men would do. He climbed onto the countertop that formed a desk in the cubicle. When the count reached zero, he jumped to his feet and aimed his rifle over the top of the wall.

At the same time, his men rushed into the ends of the aisle to prevent escape. The scratching stopped. A young woman lay half in and half out of a cubicle, her face an ashen-gray color, with blood running down the side of her head. Her fingernails dug into the carpet, probably the scratching sound they'd heard.

Dillon stood guard over the top of the wall. Chris hoisted the young woman in his arms while the other man covered him. Together they retreated toward the exit, with Dillon watching over them until they were safely out the door.

Two civilians rescued. How many more were still hiding? And where the hell was the shooter?

A soft *pfft* sound had Dillon diving to the floor and rolling into the aisle. The cubicle wall near where he'd been standing seconds ago now boasted a small round hole. A bullet hole.

"This is Gray," he whispered into his mic. "I've got gunfire on the east side, fifty feet in. Shooter's weapon is silenced." He jumped to his feet and hurried to the end of the aisle.

"Affirmative." Donna's voice came through his earpiece. "West side clear so far. Do you need backup?"

"Negative." He peeked around the wall. "Witnesses reported two shooters. Continue search and rescue on the west side. I've got this."

"You sure about that, country boy?" A gun muzzle pressed against Dillon's back.

Chapter Two

The shooter was playing a deadly game of hide-and-seek with Ashley, searching every aisle, every cubicle. So far she'd managed to stay one step ahead of him. Barely. She rounded the end of another aisle. Her breath caught in her throat. The shooter's profile was silhouetted against the wall of windows.

And his gun was pointing at a SWAT officer's back.

Ducking into the adjacent aisle, Ashley struggled to keep her breathing shallow, quiet, so the shooter wouldn't hear her. Gathering her courage, she risked another quick peek around the wall. The officer said something to the shooter. The shooter shook his head and gave him a gruff command. The officer tossed his rifle to the floor.

Dang it.

The exit door was only thirty feet away now. If Ashley was quiet, she might make it. But what would happen to the SWAT guy? He'd risked his life to rescue her and the others. Could she abandon him and leave him here to die?

No, she couldn't.

Cursing her conscience, she ducked back and grabbed one of the heavy, old-fashioned phones from a cubicle desktop. After unplugging the cord, she crept down a parallel aisle, hoping to sneak up behind the shooter. She offered up a quick prayer that he hadn't moved or turned around as she rounded the end of the row. *Yes.* His back was still facing her. But the SWAT guy was now facing the shooter, and Ashley, his hands raised.

Ashley crept forward, biting her lip, holding the phone in the air. She was pretty sure SWAT guy had seen her. He hadn't looked directly at her, but his body tensed, and the lines around his eyes tightened.

"Too bad your buddies left you by yourself," the shooter said. "Looks like they'll be carting one of their own out the door next." He raised his gun toward the officer's face just as Ashley swung the phone with both hands at the shooter's head.

But instead of hitting him, she hit empty air, spinning in a circle then falling against the wall beside her.

It took her a moment to realize SWAT guy had lunged for the shooter right when she'd swung the phone. He'd grabbed the shooter's gun and swept his legs out from beneath him. Now both men were rolling on the floor, wrestling for control of the gun.

"Get out of here," SWAT guy yelled.

Ashley realized he was yelling at her.

The two men rolled into the side aisle, grappling for control.

Leaving SWAT guy's rifle lying on the floor.

"Go, go, go," the officer yelled again. "Get out of here, run!"

SWAT guy was heavily muscled and tall, but the shooter was on top of him and must have outweighed him by at least forty pounds. The pistol was slowly, inexorably moving up toward the officer's face, the only part of his body not covered in armor.

Ashley made her choice. She dropped the phone and grabbed for the rifle.

The shooter twisted toward her and slammed his foot against her calf. She screamed and fell to the floor. Before she could scramble away, he grabbed her long hair and yanked her in front of him like a human shield.

SWAT guy crouched in the aisle a few feet away, glaring at Ashley before focusing on the shooter. The wicked-looking hunting knife in the officer's hand, along with his glare, had Ashley groaning inside. Instead of helping, she'd gotten in the way and messed everything up. She hadn't realized the policeman had a knife, and that he'd apparently been about to use it when she'd interfered.

"Let her go," the officer ordered. "You're surrounded."

Ashley glanced around, stunned to see he wasn't bluffing. She hadn't heard or seen the other SWAT officers come in, but there were two on her left, another one on the far side of the shooter and, as she watched, a fourth officer entered the aisle behind SWAT guy, who was now crouched in front of the shooter, still holding his knife.

Surrounded was putting it mildly.

"Let her go," SWAT guy repeated.

The shooter scooted back, pulling Ashley with him, keeping his gun trained on SWAT guy. Ashley struggled against his hold, but he squeezed hard, crushing her in a painful grip against his chest. He scooted back until he was pressed against the wall and couldn't move any farther.

"I'll kill her." He yanked her hair.

Ashley sucked in a sharp breath at the fiery pain.

It felt as though he was yanking half her hair out by the roots.

"Back off or she's dead. You can't shoot me without hitting her. Back. Off."

Ashley struggled to draw air into her lungs. She could barely breathe with her head twisted back so hard and tight.

Swat guy clutched his knife and motioned to the two SWAT officers on Ashley's left side. "He's right. Lower your weapons and back away. Give him room."

The shooter turned his head to the side, watching the officers lower their rifles.

He suddenly jerked against Ashley, a guttural moan wheezing out of his throat.

SWAT guy lunged forward, grabbing the shooter's gun and tossing it away. He chopped his hand down on the shooter's arm, breaking his hold on Ashley before yanking her away from him.

She twisted in the officer's arms, looking back toward the shooter. The gunman lay on the floor, convulsing, the haft of a knife sticking out of his neck. Blood bubbled out of the wound.

She clutched the officer's arm where it circled her waist.

"You—you threw your knife, while he was *holding* me?" she squeaked.

He gently grasped her chin, forcing her to turn away from the shooter.

"Look at me," he ordered, his voice gruff but laced with concern.

She dragged her gaze up his armor-covered chest to stare into a pair of stormy blue-gray eyes.

"Are you injured? Did he hurt you?" he demanded.

She swallowed and shook her head. "No. No, he

didn't… I don't think…" She shuddered. "I'm fine. He didn't hurt me."

"How many are there? Did you see any other gunmen?"

"He's the only one I saw."

He lifted her away from him. "Get her out of here."

A pair of strong arms grasped her waist and pulled her away.

Another officer hauled SWAT guy to his feet.

"Sit rep on the shooter?" he asked one of the others.

"Deceased."

SWAT guy, obviously the leader, motioned to the man holding Ashley's arm and another officer standing by the window. "Stay alert. Assume a second shooter is still in here. Get her out while we clear the rest of the building."

YELLOW CRIME-SCENE tape fluttered in the early-summer breeze, bringing with it the smell of impending rain. Ashley sat on one of the folding chairs the police had set up in the parking lot. Most of her coworkers had already been interviewed and had been allowed to leave. Ashley had been interviewed, too, but the detective who'd spoken to her had asked her to wait. She wasn't sure why.

The dead—eight in all—were still inside the building as crime scene technicians took pictures of the carnage and documented what had happened. The wounded—only three had been shot and survived—had been taken to the hospital.

The company's owner, Ron Gibson, stood talking with a couple of detectives about twenty feet away. The grief on his face reminded Ashley that he'd lost his only son today—Stanley. But Gibson was apparently a hero. He'd dragged one of the wounded out the exit before the police arrived, and he was going to be okay. The temp, whose name Ashley still couldn't remember, was also going to recover. The bullet had only grazed her head.

Another gust of wind blew through, swirling Ashley's hair. She pushed it out of her face and wished she had a ponytail holder with her. A shadow fell over her and she glanced up to see the SWAT officer who'd rescued her by throwing his knife at the shooter.

He'd shed the heavy body armor and vest with the big white letters on it marking him as SWAT. In dark blue dress pants and a white dress shirt, he could have been one of her coworkers, except that none of her coworkers were quite as muscular and fit-looking as this man. Then again, if he made his living wearing all that heavy equipment, she supposed the muscles were honestly earned.

He smiled and shook his head. "You didn't hear anything I said, did you, Miss Parrish?"

"I'm sorry, no. I was…thinking. What did you say?"

He pulled another folding chair over and sat across from her. He held out his hand and she automatically took it.

"I'm Detective Dillon Gray. I know you've already been interviewed, but I wanted to ask you a few more questions. Are you up to it?"

She shook his hand, but when he mentioned asking questions, all she could think about was the knife sticking out of the shooter's throat. She clutched his hand instead of letting go.

He didn't seem to mind. He held her hand and simply scooted his chair closer, resting his forearm across his knees.

"How long have you worked at Gibson and Gibson?"

She shook her head. "I don't work here. I mean, not for the company. I'm an independent consultant, an auditor. I work short-term contracts. I came here three weeks ago—no, four. Tomorrow…tomorrow would have been my last day." She shivered.

A look of interest lit his blue-gray eyes. "Were you brought in because of a problem? Did you find anything that concerned you when you performed the audit?"

"No, on both counts. Mr. Gibson—" she nodded toward the owner, who was being escorted to his car by one of the policemen "—he applied for a substantial loan to expand the business. The bank hired me to perform a routine audit before granting the loan. Everything checked out. I was going to recommend the loan move forward. I was supposed to finish the formal report today."

A coroner's van pulled up to the front of the building. Bile rose in Ashley's throat.

"Ignore them. Focus on me." Gray's deep voice was low and soothing, but it had the bite of authority.

She looked away from the van and met his gaze.

"I'm almost done," he said, his voice gentle. "Then you can go."

She nodded. When she heard the squeaky wheels of the coroner's gurney rolling toward the front door, she clutched his hand harder, using him as her anchor.

Another gust of wind, stronger than the rest, slapped the detective's pants against his legs. He looked up at the sky, which was casting a dark pall over the parking lot. "Looks like the weatherman was right. We're in for a heck of a storm."

He smiled at her again, and somehow the tension squeezing her chest eased, if only a little.

"I'll make this quick," he said. "You said your time here was temporary. Where's home?"

"Nashville. I've got an apartment there."

"Made any enemies in Nashville that might have come here looking for you?"

She blinked in surprise. "Me? You think the shooter was after *me,* specifically?"

"Routine questions. Just exploring all the possibilities."

The panic that had started inside her faded beneath his matter-of-fact tone. "The answer is no. I don't have any enemies. Not that I know of."

"You didn't recognize the shooter, correct?" he asked.

"I've never seen him before."

"Did he speak to you, call you by name?"

"No. He just…smiled, this really creepy, spooky smile."

His brows lowered. "What do you mean?"

"I was at the copier, with Stanley Gibson. The shooter shot Stanley, and when I turned around, he looked directly at me and…smiled. That's when I ran. I hid and kept going from aisle to aisle as he went through the room. I tried to stay a step ahead, but he caught up to me. He was on my aisle, but he was crouching down. I climbed over the wall to the next aisle before he reached my cubicle." She shivered and tugged her hand out of his grasp. The wind was colder now, making her shiver. She wrapped her arms around her middle.

Detective Gray motioned to one of the uniformed policemen nearby. "Get Miss Parrish a jacket, please."

"That's not necessary," she said. "If someone could please…get my purse…out of my cubicle inside, so I can get my car keys, I'll just go home. If you're finished with your questions?"

"By the time the officer retrieves your purse, I will be."

Ashley told the policeman where her purse was. He headed back toward the building.

"Does the name Todd Dunlop mean anything to you?" he asked.

"No. Was that the shooter's name?"

"I can't officially confirm that at this time."

"I understand. No, I've never heard that name before."

He asked her several more questions about her routine and whether she'd seen anything out of the ordinary when she got to work this morning. He asked her about any recent firings, but she wasn't aware of any.

"I'm sorry, Detective. But other than the officers of the company, I haven't even spoken to most of the people who work here. I've been stuck in a conference room most of the time, poring over years of financial reports. I wish I had better answers for you."

"You're doing fine, Miss Parrish." His white teeth flashed in a reassuring smile.

The policeman returned with her purse. She thanked him and he hurried away.

"May I go home now?" she asked the detective.

"Of course. I've got your address and your phone number. If I think of more questions, I'll stop by or give you a call. When are you leaving town?"

"The end of the week."

He walked her to her car.

She tried to unlock the car three times, but her hands were shaking so hard she couldn't get the key in the lock.

He gently took the keys from her and unlocked the door. "The clicker's broken, I assume?" He held up the electronic key fob attached to her key chain before handing back her keys.

"I think it's the battery. I keep forgetting to replace it." She slid into the driver's seat.

"You should get that fixed as soon as possible, as a security precaution," he said.

She nodded, in full agreement. After today, she was suddenly hyperaware of how dangerous the world could be. Fumbling for her keys when a simple click of a button could unlock her door didn't strike her as smart.

"Detective Gray?"

He crouched down beside her door, giving her that same kind smile he'd given her earlier. "Yes?"

"I'm sorry that I interfered, back inside. I thought I was helping, but I realize now that I could have gotten you hurt—" she swallowed hard "—or killed."

"You were very brave. You have nothing to apologize for. Everything worked out."

She offered him a shaky smile. "You saved my life. I don't know how to pay someone back for something like that."

"Fix that clicker. That's payback enough. Then I won't have to worry about you fumbling with your keys." He fished a business card out of his pocket and handed it to her. "If you think of anything else you want to tell me about what happened, anything that can help us sort through this mess and figure out why this guy picked Gibson and Gibson, give me a call."

DILLON WATCHED THE surprisingly brave, pretty little auditor drive away in her aging dark blue Chevy Lumina. He couldn't remember the last time he'd seen one of those cars on the road. Obviously Ashley Parrish wasn't making a fortune in her chosen occupation, which made any obvious financial motive for the shooter to target *her* seem unlikely.

"Did she tell you anything useful about the shooter?"

Dillon turned at the sound of Chris Downing's voice behind him.

"No. But she's pretty shaken. She might think of

something later." He glanced past his friend. His boss was standing with the rest of the SWAT team, his face animated—not in a good way—as he spoke to them. "Let me guess. Thornton sent you to get me."

"Yep. He's riled up like a preacher on Easter Sunday, all fire and brimstone raining down on our heads for going in against orders."

Dillon let out a deep sigh and started toward his boss, with Chris at his side. He wasn't in the mood to take a tongue-lashing right now, but he'd have to endure it to try to keep his job, and to keep his men from being blamed for what had essentially been a mutiny.

Regardless of the consequences, he had no regrets. The three wounded survivors they'd pulled out had lost a lot of blood and wouldn't have lasted much longer if they'd waited. And he didn't know what would have happened to Ashley Parrish. She wasn't the only survivor they'd rescued, but she was the only one the shooter had essentially stalked through the building.

Maybe he'd stop by her house on the way home tonight, to make sure she was okay and see if she'd thought of anything else that might help with the investigation. Their initial inquiries hadn't yielded any connections between the shooter and Gibson and Gibson. If the shooter had never worked there, and had never conducted any business with the company, why would he choose this particular office complex?

It was isolated, a few miles out of town, which might have made the shooter think he could shoot the place up and escape before the cops got there. But if he'd wanted to kill a lot of random people, there was a mall five minutes away that would have yielded plenty more potential victims. So why had he chosen Gibson and Gibson?

Dillon would lay odds it was something personal, and

he'd bet his ten years as a detective that the personal part was somehow related to the woman who'd just driven off in a beat-up old Chevy with a key fob that didn't work.

ASHLEY CLUTCHED HER cell phone to her ear and peered out the front window. Lightning flashed, illuminating the acres of green grass and long gravel driveway that formed the front yard of her rental house. In the distance, the Smoky Mountains loomed dark and menacing.

She'd never wanted to live this far from the conveniences in town, but her options were limited, since most people insisted on a long lease. Still, she hadn't minded living here temporarily. But with this morning's shooting fresh in her memory, the isolation was making her feel uneasy, and vulnerable.

Thunder boomed overhead.

"What was that?" Lauren asked over the phone.

"Thunder. The weathermen have been predicting a big storm all week. Looks like it's finally here. It's pitch-black outside even though it's only six o'clock. And the rain's been coming down like a monsoon for the past couple of hours. After all the rain we had last week, we sure don't need this. The river's already near flood stage."

"Should you get out of there?"

"I'll be fine. The house is on high ground and the river's several miles from here. Plus, I've stocked up on essentials in case the road gets washed out again."

Lauren droned on about poor road maintenance and the crumbling infrastructure in the country while Ashley looked through the curtains again. She would have loved to leave Destiny far behind after the horrific shooting this morning, but she'd promised Detective Gray she'd stay through the end of the week. Even if she hadn't made that promise, it would be a real pain to try to change her schedule at the last minute. She'd already planned the walk-through with her landlord so she could get her deposit back and turn in her keys.

When Lauren had called, Ashley confessed some of the general information about the shooting, but she'd kept most of the details to herself. Lauren was on a week-long cruise she'd planned for well over a year. Ashley didn't want to upset her friend and ruin her fun. She also didn't want Lauren to call Ashley's family about the shooting and get *them* upset. There'd be plenty of time to tell them what happened *after* she got back home to Nashville.

"Are you sure you're okay?" Lauren asked. "You're even quieter than usual. Maybe I should cut my vacation short and go there to be with you."

"Don't you dare. You've had this trip planned forever and I doubt they'd refund your money. Besides, by the time you got off the ship, hopped a plane, then drove forever through the boonies to get way out here, I'll be back home." She forced a note of cheerfulness she didn't feel into her voice. "Now tell me, which tropical island are you touring right now?"

Lauren hesitated, as if she was going to argue, but she finally let out a long breath. "All right, you win. I'll quit bugging you, for now. Today the cruise ship took us to a little place right outside Jamaica."

"Nice."

Lightning flashed again, much closer this time. Ashley jumped and let out a little squeak.

"Oh, yeah, you sound fine to me," Lauren accused. "Don't you want to talk about what happened?"

"Sure. Let's talk about the SWAT detective guy who rescued me. He was really hot."

"Not-so-subtle way of avoiding the topic, but I'll bite. How hot was he? Scale of one to ten."

Ashley plopped down on the couch and tucked her legs beneath her. Lauren would probably drool over Detective Dillon Gray's broad shoulders and trim waist. She'd love his dark, wavy hair that seemed a bit too long and untamed for a cop. And she'd probably squeal over what Ashley thought of as sexy stubble that formed a barely there goatee, mustache and dark shadow that ran up his jawline. He looked the way she imagined a man might look after lounging in bed with his lover for days without taking time to shave.

As enticing as all that was, Ashley knew her friend wouldn't appreciate what Ashley thought of as Dillon's best feature—his kind smile—and the gentle way he'd held her hand when she'd desperately needed the warmth and contact of another human being who wasn't trying to kill her.

He'd given her the strength to hold herself together. Without the kindness and patience he'd showed to a stranger, she probably would have lost it and imploded into a mass of nerves. Somehow, with him there, focusing those thickly lashed blue-gray eyes on her, she'd managed to keep her composure.

"Ash, come on. Scale of one to ten. Rank him."

She idly traced little circles on the arm of the couch with her fingertips as she debated her answer. If she ranked Dillon too high, Lauren would probably pester her to call him and try to wheedle a date out of him. So instead of saying "ten," which was spot-on, she lowered the number.

"A six, I suppose. It was kind of hard to tell with all that body armor on." She didn't bother to mention she'd seen him later without the armor. "Maybe a seven. Yeah, I could stretch it to a seven."

"Seven? That's not hot. That's lukewarm," Lauren scoffed. "What's his name?"

"Dillon Gray."

"Hmm. Dillon's good. Not too keen on Gray, though. Sounds kind of morose, depressing. Maybe I'll change his name when I embellish the story to my cruise ship friends at dinner."

Ashley laughed. "You do that. Oh, darn it." She jumped up from the couch and headed into the kitchen.

"What's wrong?"

She dug into the cabinet under the sink until she found a large metal mixing bowl. "Looks like that roof repair last week didn't hold. There's a healthy drip coming through the living room ceiling again."

"Dang, girl. I told you to argue with the landlord about using cheap roofers."

"I know, but I'm leaving in a few days, so what does it matter?"

"It doesn't, as long as the roof doesn't come down on you."

"Maybe it's not the roofer's fault." She placed the bowl under the leak and peered up at the plaster ceiling. "As hard as it's been raining, even a good roof might leak right now."

"You are way too nice, as always. If it were up to me, I'd call the landlord and…"

"And what?" Ashley repositioned the bowl. The drips were coming faster now. Getting some sleep tonight wasn't looking like a good prospect, not if she had to keep emptying out the water and listening to the pinging sound of the constant drips. She crossed back to the couch but paused when she realized her friend still hadn't answered.

"Lauren, are you still there?"

Silence.

She pulled the phone away and looked at the screen. Great. The call had been dropped. She plopped down on the couch and dialed Lauren's number. No ringing. Nothing. Maybe Lauren's phone wasn't the problem. She tried to get a dial tone, but it was like the phone was…dead.

Weird, that had never happened here before. The storm must have shorted something out, or maybe knocked down the nearest cell tower.

She tossed the phone down and grabbed the TV remote off the coffee table. Casting a disparaging glance at the drips rapidly filling the bowl across the room, she yanked the blanket from the back of the couch and wrapped it around her.

Thunder boomed again, this time sounding more as if it was from the back of the house than from overhead.

She paused with her finger on the remote's power button. Wait. There hadn't been any lightning that time. She slowly lowered her hand. Another sound came from behind her, down the hall.

Someone was inside the house.

Chapter Three

Dillon wrestled the steering wheel to keep his Jeep on the road. The last time he'd seen a storm this bad, the bridge over Little River washed out, stranding an entire Cub Scout troop on Cooper's Bluff, the mile-long, uninhabited island smack-dab in the middle of the river. Thankfully the mayor had learned his lesson from that fiasco. This time he'd paid attention to the weather reports and Cooper's Bluff had been evacuated earlier this afternoon, the bridge closed until the weather broke. Since the storm wasn't expected to ease until tomorrow morning, the entire police department was on standby for storm-related emergencies.

Which was why Dillon was out in the middle of the blasted thing.

This was a hell of a way to spend his evening after facing off with a crazed shooter earlier today and spending the next hour listening to his boss's tirade about chain of command and following orders. Dillon had been on the verge of telling his boss to take a hike and walking out when Thornton received his first call from the weather station, warning him the storm was going to be worse than originally thought. Thornton had immediately called for all hands on deck. Everyone had to be ready to go if and when a call for help came in.

Dillon would have rather stayed at the station and worked on the workplace-shooting investigation. But he had a four-wheel drive with a winch, which meant he was in high demand to help stranded motorists escape rapidly rising water on some of the more isolated, two-lane roads. He'd spent the past six hours pulling half a dozen vehicles out of swollen ditches. Now his shoulders and back ached and all he wanted to do was pop the top on an ice-cold beer, lie down in his recliner and sleep.

The squawk of his cell phone had him clenching the steering wheel even harder. He ignored the first ring, irrationally hoping whoever was calling would call someone else instead, preferably someone who hadn't been working solid since sunup and was bone weary.

But when the phone rang again, his shoulders slumped and he answered, "Gray."

"Detective Gray, this is Nancy, nine-one-one operator. I have Lauren Wilkes on the line. She specifically asked to speak to you. Something about her friend possibly being in trouble. Should I patch her through?"

Dillon let out a long sigh. That cold beer would have to wait a little bit longer. "Go ahead, Nancy. Thanks."

"Pleasure."

The line clicked twice.

"Miss Wilkes, Detective Gray is on the line," the operator said. "Go ahead with your emergency."

"Emergency? Well, ah, yes. Thank you." The young woman's voice sounded nervous. "Detective Gray? Are you there?"

"I'm here. How can I help you?"

"I feel a little silly. I'm not sure anything is really wrong, but after what happened this morning I'm kind of nervous. I mean, there's the storm and all and maybe phones do that sometimes but I remember she told me your name and so when—"

"Miss Wilkes," Dillon interrupted. "Take a breath."

"What? Oh, yes. Okay."

"Tell me why you called." He pulled the Jeep to the side of the road. It was too dangerous trying to talk on the phone and fight the wheel in this wind and rain.

"It's my friend. I was talking to her and the phone went dead. I tried calling her back, over and over, but the call doesn't go through. I was wondering if you could check on her. I'm, ah, not close by, so it's not like I can hop in the car and go over there."

Dillon thumped his forehead on the steering wheel. "Ma'am, if the Smoky Mountains were by the ocean I'd call the storm we're in right now a hurricane. Storms this bad always knock landlines down."

"Oh, well, it's not a landline. It's her cell phone. Do storms knock those out, too?"

He straightened in his seat. "Not usually, no. I suppose something could have happened to a cell tower." Although he couldn't remember that ever happening around here before. He grabbed the notebook and pen lying in the console. "What's your friend's name and address? I'll do a wellness check for you."

"Oh, would you, please? That would be awesome. And if you'll call me back and let me know she's okay, I'd really appreciate it. I mean, we've been friends forever. I kind of get worried—"

"Ma'am, the name and address?"

"Oh, right. Sorry. She's renting a house at 1010 Little River Road. Her name is Ashley Parrish."

Dillon stiffened. Every cell in his body went on alert. Cell phone towers could go out, he supposed, but it was a hell of a coincidence for that to happen to the woman who'd survived a workplace shooting just this morning. He tossed the notebook and pen in the console and whipped the Jeep back onto the road.

"Tell me everything that happened," he said, fighting to keep the vehicle straight as he jostled the phone and headed back toward Little River Road. Ashley's house was only five minutes away. "Don't leave anything out."

In the rough weather, it took six minutes instead of the normal five to reach the right road, and another two minutes to reach the long, winding driveway that led to Ashley's house.

A few inches of water covered most of the gravel, but his four-wheel drive clung to the road like a billy goat. He parked next to the front porch steps, figuring he'd save himself some soggy boots by avoiding the puddles in the yard.

He shook the raindrops from the last outing into the storm off his ball cap, shoved it on his head and threw the car door open. He slammed it shut behind him and jogged up the steps. Lights were on inside. He rapped on the front door. A few seconds later he rapped again, and rang the doorbell.

Nothing.

"Miss Parrish?" he called out. "It's Detective Gray. We met this morning. I need to speak to you." Another knock, but again, no sound or movement from inside.

The mild alarm he'd felt after talking to Lauren Wilkes was giving way to genuine concern. The little hairs on his neck were standing up. He drew his gun and held it down by his side as he stepped to the front window. He could glimpse the room through a slit in the curtains, but not enough to really tell him anything.

His boots echoed hollowly on the wood as he strode

across the porch. At the corner of the house, he leaned around, looking toward the backyard. Pitch-dark. The landlord needed to get some lights out here, especially since the house was so isolated without any neighbors close by. He headed back to the steps to get a flashlight from his Jeep so he could walk the perimeter of the property.

The sound of a powerful engine had him jerking around.

Headlights flashed and a truck roared from the side yard. It raced past him, its tires throwing up huge sprays of water that splashed onto the porch.

There were two people in the truck. The passenger turned and looked right at him, her eyes wide, her face pale as her hands flailed ineffectually against the glass.

Ashley Parrish.

She definitely wasn't in that truck because she *wanted* to be.

Dillon crouched on the porch and fired off two quick shots at the truck's tires, hoping to disable it before it gained much speed.

The truck jerked to the side but kept going. Damn this rain and wind. He wouldn't normally miss a shot like that. Taking the stairs two at a time, he hopped into his car, wheeled it around and floored the accelerator.

The Jeep fishtailed on the wet gravel. Dillon cursed and let up on the gas, then took off at a slower speed. The headlights from the truck bounced crazily as it turned at the end of the drive. West, it was heading west.

He grabbed his phone and pressed the button for dispatch as he barreled down the driveway. Nothing. He held the phone up. The light was on and he'd pressed the right button, but the call hadn't gone through. Must be the bad cell tower, as he'd thought earlier.

After making the turn at the end of the drive onto the paved road, he floored the gas again. The truck's taillights were barely visible up ahead in the pouring rain. There weren't any streetlights out on this old rural two-lane. But he didn't need more than his headlights to tell him what he already knew. The road up ahead was full of dangerous, sharp S-curves. If the driver of that truck kept his current speed, on this slick, wet road, he'd likely end up in a ditch or plow headfirst into a tree.

ASHLEY CLUNG TO the armrest and braced her other hand against the dashboard. The rain was falling so hard the windshield wipers couldn't keep up. The truck's tires kept slipping on the wet road, making the bottom drop out of her stomach.

"Please slow down," she pleaded. "It's too dangerous to drive this fast in these conditions."

The driver raised his gun and pointed it at her without taking his gaze from the road.

She swallowed and held her hands up in a placating gesture.

He shoved the gun between his legs and put both hands back on the wheel, the veins in his forearms bulging from the effort it took to keep the truck on the road.

Ashley glanced in the side mirror. The lights from Dillon Gray's Jeep were barely visible in the distance, but he was steadily gaining on them. She didn't have a clue why he'd gone to her house, but he was the answer to her prayers. If he could catch up and somehow manage to get this eerily calm stranger to stop the truck…

She let out a yelp as the truck slid toward the ditch on their right.

Her captor let up on the gas. The wheels caught and spit the truck back toward the middle of the road.

DILLON'S HEART PLUMMETED as the black pickup carrying Ashley Parrish slid dangerously close to the edge of the road for the second time since he'd started pursuit. At the last second, the truck straightened out and shot back toward the centerline.

He let out a pent-up breath and pushed his Jeep even harder, the engine whining as it struggled to catch up. His four-wheel drive was built for power, not speed, which was why he didn't normally use it when on the job. And it wasn't aerodynamic enough to make the curves without greatly reducing his speed. Neither was the truck up ahead. The ditches along this road might as well be cliffs, as steep as they were. And with all this rain, they were full of water, a death trap if the truck slid into one of them.

He tried his phone again, but it was no use. He no longer believed a failed cell tower was to blame. He'd gone too far from Ashley's house for that to be the case. The driver of the truck had to have a powerful cell phone jammer. That would explain why Ashley's call dropped when she was talking to her friend, and why Dillon couldn't get a call through as he followed behind. His mouth tightened. Jammers weren't cheap, and they were hard to come by. The man who'd taken Ashley had gone to a lot of trouble, and expense, to do it. This wasn't a random abduction.

He debated pulling off the road to call dispatch for backup. But if he let enough distance pass between him and the truck to unblock his phone, he might lose their trail. He couldn't risk it.

The road curved ahead, but no matter how hard Dillon pressed his Jeep on the straightaway, he couldn't catch up before the pickup disappeared around the curve. When he rounded the bend, he slammed his fist against the steering wheel. The fool. The truck's lights were visible up ahead, but not on the two-lane it had been on. Instead, the driver had turned down the side road that led to Cooper's Bluff. And he was heading toward the low wooden bridge over Little River—the bridge the mayor had closed because the river was expected to top it.

Ignoring every sense of self-preservation he had, he pushed the accelerator all the way to the floor. The tires slipped. He cursed and let up on the gas, even though it nearly killed him to slow down.

The bridge was around the next curve, so he slowed the Jeep even more.

Taillights gleamed up ahead at a crazy angle.

Dillon's eyes widened and he slammed the brakes, bringing his car to a skidding halt at the edge of the roadway. The last twenty feet of asphalt had washed away. The bridge was completely underwater, its support beams sticking up out of the angry, roiling waves like the skeleton of some prehistoric water beast. The truck had slid off the collapsed roadway, narrowly missing the bridge's first support beam and sliding half into the river.

Dillon grabbed his flashlight and hopped out. He sprinted to what was now little more than a cliff, a fifteen-foot drop down to the strip of mud at the water's edge. The front of the truck was submerged beneath the water, all the way up to the doors. The bed of the truck stuck up in the air, and even as Dillon watched, the truck slipped a few more inches into the water.

He took off, racing parallel to the shore until he found a break where he could climb down. His boots slipped and slid in the muddy, rain-soaked ground.

In the beam of his flashlight he saw Ashley frantically tugging at her seat belt, her frightened eyes pleading with him for help as the water sucked and pulled at the truck. Dillon waded waist deep into the churning water to get to her door. The window was still rolled up, probably electric and stuck. He looked past her. The driver appeared to be passed out over the wheel. A rivulet of blood ran down the side of his face.

Ashley managed to get her seat belt off and yanked the door handle, but it wouldn't open against the current. She pounded the flats of her hands against the window.

"Turn away from the glass," Dillon yelled.

When Ashley moved back, Dillon used the hard case of his flashlight like a hammer against the window. It bounced and thudded against the glass. He tried again and again but the glass still held.

The truck slid deeper into the water.

Ashley screamed.

The driver stirred beside her.

Dillon shoved the flashlight under his arm and pulled out his gun.

"I have to shoot the window out," he yelled.

She nodded, letting him know she understood. She pulled her legs up onto the seat, squeezing back from the window.

Dillon aimed toward the corner, so his bullet would go into the dashboard, and squeezed the trigger.

The safety glass shattered but held. He slammed the butt of his gun against the window. This time it collapsed in a shower of tiny glass pieces. He started to shove his gun into his holster but Ashley dove at him in the window opening, knocking both the flashlight and the pistol into the boiling, raging water.

He grabbed her beneath her arms and pulled.

She screamed.

He froze, horrified that he might have cut her on the glass.

"Let me go. Let me go," she screamed again. But she wasn't talking to him.

Dillon looked past her into the steady, dark eyes of the driver. He had a hold of Ashley's waist and was playing a deadly game of tug-of-war.

"Let her go," Dillon yelled. "I'll pull her out, then come back for you. The truck's back wheels aren't going to hold much longer."

"We'll take our chances in the river." The man's voice was deadly calm, as if he wasn't the least bit concerned. He heaved backward, pulling Ashley farther into the truck, slamming Dillon against the door. His grip slipped.

Ashley frantically flailed her arms. He reached for her and grabbed her hands.

The wheels made a great big sucking noise as they popped free from the mud. Ashley's hands were yanked out of Dillon's wet grasp. The truck went twisting and floating down the rain-swollen river, with Ashley's terrified screams echoing back, tearing at Dillon's heart.

The normally calm river was now a dangerous cauldron of rapids and swirling currents. The truck wouldn't stay afloat for long. Even if Ashley made it out and into the water, she wouldn't survive. No one could swim in that current. Only a fool would go into the river now.

He cursed and tore off his jacket. Apparently, he was a fool.

He dove into the river.

Chapter Four

Another wave crashed over Dillon's head, shoving him back under like a waterlogged towel tossed in a giant washing machine. His lungs burned. His muscles ached from fighting against the current.

He kicked his legs and clawed his way toward the barely discernible sliver of moonlight that told him which direction was up. He burst to the surface, gulping air into his lungs. Lightning flashed in the sky, followed by a boom of thunder so loud it hurt his ears. The rain pummeled his skin like hundreds of tiny icy needles.

Another wave crashed down. Again he went under. Again he fought his way back up for another precious lungful of air. He'd lost sight of the truck. And he wasn't trying to swim in any particular direction anymore.

He was just trying to survive.

It was too dark to see more than a few feet in front of him. He didn't know where he was, or even if he was within reach of land. His muscles screamed for relief, cried out for rest. He couldn't keep fighting much longer.

Moonlight glinted off the whitecap of another wall of water rushing toward him. He inhaled deeply just as the wave slammed into him. Like a spear in his chest, the water pushed him down, down, down until he bumped against the muddy bottom of the river.

The pressure pinned him against a rock. He latched onto it, fire lancing through his lungs as he waited for the current to shift. His vision blurred. The irony that he might actually drown suddenly struck him as funny. A laugh erupted from him, sending a froth of bubbles up toward the surface. His lungs protested the loss of desperately needed oxygen.

He pictured the fireplace mantel in his parents' farmhouse, still filled with his decade-old swim trophies from high school, like open wounds that had never healed. What would his mother do when she heard her swim-champion son had drowned? Would she throw away the trophies that had made her so proud? Would she hate him for giving up?

He clenched the rock harder. Tired, so tired. All he had to do was open his mouth and take a deep gulp of water and it would be over. He wouldn't have to fight anymore. His eyes drifted closed. The last of his air bubbled out of his nose. He sank deeper against the rock.

The image of his mother's face drifted through his thoughts, surprising him with the anger in her faded blue eyes. She reached out, but instead of hugging him goodbye, she grabbed his shoulders and shook him.

She needs you. Help her.

His mother's face faded, replaced by Ashley Parrish's wide-eyed stare, her scream of terror as the truck went into the river.

Dillon's eyes flew open. He couldn't give up. Not yet. He had to try. One more time.

He let the rock go and pushed toward the moonlight again. Up, up, up. He broke the surface, inhaling deeply. The rush of air into his starved lungs was painful, like the rush of blood into a circulation-starved limb. He ducked beneath the next wave and came right back up this time. He was used to swimming in pools or the pond on his parents' farm, not this roiling nightmare that pounded at him and made his muscles shake with exhaustion.

Maybe that was the problem. He was fighting too hard. He thought back to the basics, something his first swim coach had taught him, something he'd never had use for. Until now. Dead man float. He dodged the next wave, gulped in a deep breath, another.

Then he stopped fighting.

Lying facedown in the water, he held his hands out in front of him to protect his head from any debris. He held his breath, no longer struggling against a monster he couldn't defeat, and let the current take him wherever it wanted as the freezing rain beat down on his back. He jerked his head out of the water, took another breath, relaxed again. Over and over he repeated the routine—breathe, relax, float, breathe, relax, float.

His arm banged against something hard and unyielding. The current shoved him against a solid object—the truck, tangled up in a downed tree at the edge of the river.

The powerful current tugged at him, trying to pull him back out. His wet hands flailed against the slippery metal. He kicked hard and slammed into the bumper. Latching on, he stubbornly refused to let go. Hand over hand, using the bumper like a towline, he carefully inched his way down the end of the truck.

His kicking feet struck bottom. He pushed, his calf muscles burning from exertion as he fought his way to the driver's door. Waves pummeled his back. He coughed up a lungful of water and kept pushing, one step at a time.

The rain wouldn't let up, and as more and more of Dillon's body rose up out of the water, he began to shiver. His teeth chattered so hard he wondered they didn't chip or break.

When he finally reached the door, he saw what he'd already suspected. The cab was empty. Had Ashley made it out alive? What about the man who'd abducted her?

That thought drove him harder, through the shallows toward land.

He wanted to curse and rail at the storm mercilessly pounding against him, and the sucking current trying to pull him away from shore. Every inch, every step, was a hard-fought victory. But he didn't say the foul words he wanted to say. He made as little noise as he could, because he didn't know if the man who'd taken Ashley was within earshot, perhaps waiting in the trees up ahead.

Hoping the dark, nearly moonless night would help conceal him, he struggled on. Past the truck now, clinging to the branches of the tree that had snared the vehicle. He pulled himself out of the water and collapsed on the muddy bank. If the kidnapper found him now, Dillon didn't think he could do anything to defend himself. He was limp and spent.

Shivering in the mud, he lay there, gasping in precious air, trying to gather his strength. It was the icy rain, painfully stabbing the skin on his exposed arms, that finally made him move. He crawled forward, forcing one knee in front of the other until he reached the cover of trees. Using the low-hanging branch of a pine tree for leverage, he pulled himself to his feet.

Where was he? He couldn't seem to get his bearings.

A flash of lightning lit the sky, making everything as bright as daylight for a split second, just long enough for him to see his Jeep parked at the drop-off where the bridge used to be.

On the other side of the river.

He was on Cooper's Bluff, with no weapons, no phone and no way off the island—presumably with an armed man holding a woman hostage.

Some days it didn't pay to even put his boots on in the morning.

He shoved off the tree and trudged deeper into the forest, his weary legs shaking beneath him. It was damned embarrassing how much the freezing water had taken out of him. Thankfully, none of his men were there to see his sorry state.

A muted yell sounded from somewhere deep in the woods.

Dillon stiffened and tried to pinpoint the direction the sound had come from. A scream jolted him into action. His misery and exhaustion forgotten, he plunged into the trees at a full-out run.

ASHLEY HELD HER hand to her aching jaw and warily eyed the man who'd knocked her to the ground. Biting his arm wasn't the smartest decision she'd ever made.

He towered over her, but it wasn't his height or his brawny build that held her attention. It was the gun in his hand, the business end pointing straight at her head. She'd wondered why he hadn't immediately chased her when the truck snagged in the tree and she dove out the window. Now she knew. He'd fished out the gun from the floorboard where it had fallen when the truck first went into the water.

Would it fire now that it was wet? The way her luck had gone today, she was betting it would.

He squatted down in front of her, the gun never wavering. Cold rain dripped through the thick foliage overhead, splashing onto his forearms. But he didn't seem to notice. If he had yelled at her, it would have been far less frightening than the emotionless, dead look in his eyes. She mentally dubbed him Iceman, because he was so cold, as if he had no soul.

"Miss Parrish, bite me again and the next time I hit you you'll be missing half your teeth." He motioned toward her feet. "Take off your shoes."

She frowned down at her sneakers. The idea of walking through the cold, soggy, rock-strewn forest without protection on her feet didn't appeal to her in the least. "My shoes?"

"I'm not in the habit of repeating myself."

"I don't understand. Why do you want—"

He backhanded her, sending her sprawling onto the ground.

A yelp of pain escaped between her clenched teeth. He grabbed one of her feet and yanked off her shoe. Before she could get away from him, he yanked off her other shoe. When he let her go, she scrambled back like a crab on all fours. She cast a furtive glance around, looking for some kind of weapon. All she saw were small, round river rocks. Pelting him with those would be like poking an angry bull with a toy spear.

Iceman jerked at the laces on her confiscated shoes, yanking them out of the eyelets.

A feeling of dread swept through Ashley. There was only one reason she could think of that he'd want those laces. To tie her up.

She scrambled to her feet to run into the trees behind her.

"I need you alive," his voice echoed, freezing her in place. "But you don't need kneecaps to live. Sit your butt back down."

She sucked in a sharp breath and plopped on the ground. "Who are you? Why are you doing this?"

"Hold out your hands." He squatted down in front of her again with one of the shoelaces.

It was so tempting to take advantage of his vulnerable position and turn him into a soprano, but without shoes she wasn't sure she could kick him hard enough to risk another swing of his fist. She was also rather fond of her kneecaps.

She grudgingly held out her hands.

The wet lace bit into her left wrist as he yanked it tight. He was just as rough with her right wrist, painfully tightening the shoelace against her skin, jerking it to ensure it wouldn't slip off. He knotted the two laces together, forcing her to lock her fingers in a two-handed fist to relieve the pressure.

"Police," a voice yelled behind him. "Put your hands above your head and lie facedown on the ground."

She sucked in a breath and stared past her captor. The silhouette of another man was visible about ten feet away. Lightning briefly lit the clearing, revealing his identity—Detective Dillon Gray.

His wet hair was plastered to his scalp and his Kevlar vest formed a dark shadow beneath his equally wet shirt. Her mouth dropped open. Did he actually *swim* across the swollen, raging river to rescue her? Shock and gratitude warred with disbelief. But any relief she felt turned to worry when she realized one thing—*he didn't have a weapon.*

Iceman wrapped his fingers around the gun shoved in his belt. Did he know the police officer behind him was bluffing?

Ashley stared into his dark eyes. They were no longer cold and dead. Instead, they shined with an unholy gleam and his mouth tilted in anticipation.

He knew. He knew Dillon didn't have a gun. He must have seen it fall into the river when Dillon was trying to pull Ashley out the truck window.

"Move away from her and lie on the ground. Now," the detective repeated, his deep voice authoritative and confident.

The cord of muscles in Iceman's thick neck pulsed, reminding her of a snake coiling to strike.

She whipped a glance at the detective, trying to warn him with her eyes. But it was so dark. He probably couldn't see her eyes any better than she could see his.

A vile curse flashed through her mind, the kind of curse that would have had her mama looking for the biggest, thickest switch she could find, if she ever actually heard Ashley say it—regardless of how old Ashley was.

The detective was a big man, tall and thick with muscles, but just like at the Gibson and Gibson office building, the thug he was facing was even bigger. Dillon had come out the winner in the earlier confrontation, but he'd had a weapon, and a team of officers to distract the bad guy.

The man crouching in front of Ashley had the only advantage that mattered right now. A gun. One little bullet was all it would take to end this standoff. Even if the vest protected Dillon, the force of the bullet would probably knock him flat on his back. Then all the gunman had to do was calmly stand over Dillon and shoot him in the head.

She needed to do something. But what? The last time she'd interfered with this same police officer she'd nearly gotten him killed.

Suddenly the gunman whirled around.

As if anticipating the move, Dillon lunged to the side. He rolled out of the way and scrambled to his feet.

Bam, bam— Iceman fired off two quick shots, flames shooting out of the muzzle like a warning flare.

Dillon grunted and fell to the ground. His body jerked, then lay still.

Ashley's nails bit into the backs of her tied fists. She silently urged Dillon to move, to run, but he lay face-down on the ground—stunned, or worse.

The gunman stalked toward him.

Ashley frantically looked around. There had to be *something* she could use as a weapon. But even though the icy rain was still dripping through the heavy canopy overhead, and the wind clacked the branches against each other, there wasn't even a large twig on the ground anywhere within reach.

Thunder sounded. Lightning lit up the clearing, illuminating Dillon. He still wasn't moving.

Oh, dear God, no.

Ashley jumped to her feet. If nothing else, she could swing her tied fists at the gunman and try to knock his gun out of his hand before he could shoot Dillon again. She charged forward.

The gunman stopped beside Dillon and raised his gun.

Ashley pulled her tied hands back like a bat to swing at him. Dillon suddenly jerked to the side and kicked Iceman's legs, knocking him to the ground. Ashley yelped and scrambled out of the way. The two men grappled with each other, locked in combat.

The storm was getting worse. Sheets of rain pelted them through the gaps in the trees. Ashley shoved her wet hair out of her face. Lightning cracked overhead in short bursts, a strobe light revealing the men's movements every few seconds, like a projector showing every other frame in a movie.

They rolled back and forth, grunting, twisting as they each strained for the advantage over the other. One of them got his arm free and swung his fist with massive force against the other man's jaw. A loud crack echoed in the clearing. His opponent screamed and fell to the side, clutching his face, shaking his head as if in a daze.

The victor climbed to his feet. Moonlight glinted off the gun in his hand.

Ashley pressed her hand to her throat. Who was lying on the ground? And who was holding the gun? Lightning flashed again, revealing the face of the man who was standing. Ashley's shoulders slumped with relief.

"I'm Detective Dillon Gray. You're under arrest," he gasped between deep breaths. His chest heaved from exertion, but the gun never wavered in his grip. "What's your name?"

The other man shook his head again, as if trying to get his bearings. He rubbed his jaw and glared up at Dillon while climbing to his feet. He staggered at first and then straightened to his full height, several inches taller than Dillon.

Thunder boomed, startling Ashley, but Dillon didn't even flinch.

"Your name," he demanded again, but the other man remained mute.

"Miss Parrish," Dillon said. "Get behind me. Make a wide berth around this gentleman, please."

Staying well away from her abductor, she hurried to

the other side of the clearing. Iceman's head swiveled, following her every move, like the sights on a rifle. She thanked God it was too dark for her to see the look in those creepy dead eyes. She stopped beside Dillon, but he shoved her behind him.

"Facedown, on the ground," he ordered the other man.

Ashley peeked around Dillon's broad shoulders. Her abductor wasn't cooperating. Instead of getting down, he braced his feet wide apart.

"Ah, hell," Dillon said.

Ashley clutched the back of his shirt. "Can't you just…shoot him?"

"I'd certainly like to, but my boss frowns on shooting unarmed civilians."

Iceman grinned, his teeth flashing in the moonlight like a wolf baring its fangs.

"That doesn't mean I won't," Dillon warned him. "If you take a single step, I'll shoot. I'm too exhausted for another boxing round and I'm freezing. Not to mention I have a civilian to protect. I *will* shoot if you force my hand. Get down on the ground. Now."

The man's grin faded. Ashley couldn't see well enough to identify the expression on his face, but judging by the way his shoulders stiffened, she'd bet he was considering charging the detective. If *she* had a gun, she wouldn't wait for the bad guy to make a decision. She'd shoot, right now. This man had already attacked both of them. If he got another chance, she had no doubt he'd do it again.

"Who are you?" Dillon repeated. "Why are you after Miss Parrish?"

"He said he needed me alive," Ashley said.

Dillon digested that for a moment. “Have you ever fired a gun?”

“Me?” she squeaked.

He sighed. “I guess that’s a no. There’s no safety. All you do is point and squeeze. I want you to point my gun directly at our guest while I handcuff him. If he moves, squeeze the trigger. Can you do that?”

“I’d have no trouble shooting this jerk. He stole my shoes,” she said.

His mouth twitched, as if he was trying not to laugh. “If I didn’t have to keep this gun trained on this fellow I’d cut those laces with my pocketknife. But I don’t want to risk cutting you. Hold your hands up and I’ll untie them.”

She held her clasped hands on his left side while he kept his gun trained on the quiet, deadly stranger with his right hand.

He plucked at the laces, mostly by feel, and soon they were loose enough so she could unclasp her hands.

“I can get it the rest of the way.” She worked the laces free and dropped them to the forest floor. Rubbing her aching wrists, she glared at the man responsible. Her glare was probably wasted since it was so dark, but it made her feel better.

“Okay, I’m ready,” she said.

Dillon kept his gun trained on the other man while he pulled out a set of handcuffs from a holder on his belt.

“Mister, I strongly suggest you cooperate. If you lie still while I put the cuffs on, you won’t get shot. But if you try anything, Miss Parrish seems quite anxious to repay you for her ill use tonight.”

The man hesitated, then got down on his knees and lowered himself to the ground. He lay with his head to the side, watching both of them as he put his arms behind his back.

Dillon cursed softly beneath his breath.

"What's wrong?" Ashley whispered.

"That was way too easy."

"You think he's planning something?"

"I think he plans to fight me again. He's assuming you won't shoot."

"But I will. I promise."

His mouth twitched again. "Actually, I'd prefer you don't, since you've never fired a gun before," he whispered. "I don't want to get shot again. I'm already a walking bruise. We'll bluff, but don't shoot unless your own life is in danger. I repeat, do *not* shoot when I'm anywhere near him." He handed her the gun, keeping it pointed at the other man.

She tightened her fingers around the grip. It was heavier than she'd expected. Her hands dipped beneath the weight. He grabbed her wrists and steadied the gun.

"Like this." He adjusted her hold, making the gun more balanced. She nodded to let him know she had it this time.

"Only shoot as a last resort," he whispered again. "To save *yourself*."

"All right," she assured him. But she had no intention of doing *nothing* if Iceman tried something. If it came down to it, she *would* shoot, but she didn't tell Dillon that. He seemed too worried she'd shoot *him*. It was a bit insulting, really. How hard could it be to aim and pull a trigger from ten feet away?

He moved forward, keeping well clear of the other man's legs. He suddenly dropped down with his knee in the small of the man's back. At the same time he twisted the man's arms up between his shoulder blades.

Iceman let out a low roar of rage. Whatever he'd planned to do was a moot point now. Dillon had immobilized him before he could even move. Ashley was thoroughly impressed.

Dillon snapped the cuff around one of the man's massive wrists.

A loud boom echoed through the trees. Dillon stiffened and fell to the side, landing hard on the ground with a pained grunt.

A bald-headed man ran out of the woods holding a gun. Iceman jumped up from the ground, the handcuffs dangling from his left wrist.

Ashley aimed at Baldy and squeezed the trigger. The gun boomed and jerked in her hands. She fell back on her butt in the mud. *Dang it.* She twisted to the side and scrambled to her feet, expecting to feel the bite of Baldy's bullet any second.

But Baldy didn't have his gun anymore. Iceman had it. Somehow her shot, instead of hitting the bald man, had hit Iceman in the shoulder. Blood ran down his arm and dripped from his limp fingers. He must have taken the gun from his partner, because he glared at Ashley and started to raise his other hand, the one now holding the gun.

She braced her legs so she wouldn't fall back this time and squeezed the trigger again and again and again. Both men shouted and dove to the ground. They took off running into the woods.

An arm snaked around her waist and the gun was plucked from her hands.

She jerked against her captor and tried to twist in his arms to get the gun back.

"Stop fighting me." Dillon's harsh command sounded near her ear. She hadn't even seen him get up off the ground.

She blew out a relieved breath and stopped struggling. He let her go and she turned to face him. "I did really good! I scared them both away."

"You scared all of us the way your bullets were ricocheting around the clearing. I told you not to shoot."

"You're welcome," she grumbled. The least the man could do was be grateful since she'd probably saved his life. Her gaze dipped to his chest and she gasped at the sight of two bullet holes in his shirt. "That man shot you." She ran her hands over the fabric, feeling the vest beneath. "Did the vest stop the bullets? Did the other guy shoot you, too? Are you okay?" She trailed her fingers to his sides and then down his arms.

He sucked in a breath and plucked her hands off him. "I'm okay." His eyes widened and he stared past her across the dark clearing. "We can't catch a break, can we? I hear them. They're coming back. How much do you want to bet they probably *both* have guns this time?"

He grabbed her hand and tugged her toward the trees behind him.

One of her bare feet came down on a hard rock. She yelped and tugged her hand out of his grasp. "My shoes. I need my shoes. They're back over—"

The wood exploded on the tree by her right leg and a deafening boom echoed through the clearing.

Ashley took off running, leaving Dillon to chase after her.

Chapter Five

"Why are we stopping?" Ashley tried to say, but it came out more like "wwwwhy are wwweee stoppp-piiinng" between her chattering, clenched teeth. The cold wouldn't have bothered her so much if she wasn't cold *and* wet. And she had a stitch in her side from running so long and so hard over rough terrain. She clutched the nearest tree for support and drew deep, gasping breaths while trying to will away the painful ache in her side.

She certainly didn't mind stopping—that wasn't why she'd asked the question. She'd like nothing more than to curl into a tight ball on the forest floor and give her aching muscles a rest, in spite of the incessant rain still coming down. But she also didn't want to give their pursuers a chance to catch up to them.

Dillon didn't spare her more than a quick glance. He slid the clip out of the gun and checked it, then slid it back in until it clicked. He stood protectively in front of her, peering into the gloom surrounding them. The darkness would have been welcome under the circumstances, since it helped conceal them, but lightning kept flashing overhead like a spotlight.

"Why did we stop?" she repeated, proud she'd managed to speak coherently this time without her teeth chattering. She impatiently shoved her wet hair out of her eyes.

"We're almost at the end of the island." His voice was pitched low. "If we keep running, we'll end up in the river. We'll have to double back, find somewhere to shelter and take a stand." He glanced at her. "Besides, your feet are a bloody mess. The only reason you're still able to run is because the cold has made you numb."

She lifted one of her feet, gasping when she saw the blood. He was right. She hadn't even felt the pain. But of course, now that he'd mentioned it, her feet started throbbing.

"Okay, ouch. But it doesn't matter. We have to keep going. I'd really love *not* to get shot today."

Amusement lit his eyes and he raised a brow.

Her face flushed hot. "Yes, I know. *You've* been shot, what, two, three times? I'm really, *really* sorry about that."

He let out a puff of laughter. "You're not the only one." He absently rubbed his chest as if it pained him and scanned the trees again. Seemingly satisfied, he shoved his gun in his waistband, then pulled his shirt off over his head.

Ashley blinked in surprise, and her mouth suddenly watered in appreciation. The bulletproof vest hid much of his chest, but his bulging biceps were now displayed for her viewing pleasure. She'd always been a sucker for muscles and golden skin, and Dillon's arms were like a sculpted work of art. Her fingers itched with the desire to slide over that smooth skin, up his arms, over his broad shoulders to sink into his thick, dark hair. How good would it feel to have those strong arms close around her and cradle her to his chest? What would the rest of his body look like without the armor? Would it be as enticing as she imagined? Or even better?

A ripping sound had her blinking again. She'd zoned out, fixating on totally inappropriate thoughts given their circumstances. She blamed her lack of focus on blood loss from her injured feet. Dillon, thankfully, didn't seem to have noticed her distraction. He was too busy cutting strips off his shirt with a pocketknife.

"Detective Gray—"

"Dillon."

"Dillon, it's cold out here. And it's still raining. Or hadn't you noticed?"

"I did notice, actually. Especially since I swam in a freezing-cold river to get here."

She winced. "I never thanked you for that. Thanks."

He smiled. "We've both been a bit busy. And to answer your next question, the reason I took my shirt off and am currently destroying it is because I'm going to use these strips to wrap your feet." He put his knife away and waved at a fallen tree a few feet away, indicating for her to sit.

Normally, she'd decline the offer to sit on a half-rotted, probably bug-infested dead tree, but ever since he'd mentioned the cuts on her feet, they were stinging and throbbing. She gratefully plopped down.

Dillon crouched beside her with the cloth strips from his ruined shirt.

"Miss Parrish—"

"Detective Gray?"

He smiled. "Is that a hint to call you by your first name?"

"Nothing gets by you."

His grin widened before fading away all too quickly. "Ashley, other than your feet, are you okay? When I first reached the island, I heard you scream. Did he… Did that man…hurt you?"

Her face heated at his intent look, and the obvious meaning behind his question. He wanted to know if she'd been raped. She swallowed hard, only now realizing how *lucky* she'd been tonight. With all the awful things that had happened, it could have been so much worse.

"No," she quietly assured him, "he didn't hurt me. Not the way you mean, at least. He backhanded me across the face. Twice. But nothing else."

He frowned and studied her face. Lightning flashed, and he feathered his fingers across her cheek and jaw where the man had hit her. In spite of the gentleness of his touch, pain lanced through her jaw beneath his fingers. She drew in a sharp breath.

He dropped his hand. "Sorry. Nothing appears to be broken, but you're definitely going to have a couple of good bruises in the morning. Your cheek and jaw are already swelling. Unfortunately, there isn't much I can do about that. But I *can* wrap your feet."

"I'm not worried about my feet right now," she insisted, only half lying because it felt so good *not* to be standing on her aching feet. "Those men could be anywhere. We need to get moving again."

"You don't think I know that? You're leaving a blood trail that will be far too easy to follow when the sun comes up. We have to staunch the blood."

Her lips formed a silent "oh" and she dutifully lifted her left foot when he reached for it. She felt like a child who'd been reprimanded. Or a civilian who'd been reminded by a cop that he knew what he was doing.

Obviously, he *did* know, or she'd have been dead several times over today.

She sucked in a breath when he wrapped the strips of cloth around her foot. The pressure sent sharp, stinging pains zinging up her legs.

"Detective…Dillon, how did you find me? I mean, why did you come to my house tonight in the first place?"

"Your friend Lauren Wilkes was worried about you when she couldn't get a call through. I guess the shooting this morning had her spooked, so she called nine-one-one. It's a good thing she did." His movements were quick and economical, as if he'd done something like this many times before, and soon both feet were bandaged.

"Yes, it is. I'll have to thank her later. Assuming we make it off this island."

"Don't you worry. We'll make it." Straightening, he pulled the gun out again and held it down by his side. "I grew up around here. I know every inch of Cooper's Bluff. There are some caves where we can probably hole up for the night. It's a defensible position, probably the only one on the island. But it's a ten-minute hike from here." He looked down at her feet. "Maybe fifteen. Think you can make it?"

A thrashing sound echoed through the trees, faint, but definitely getting closer.

Defensible position sounded ominous to her, but those sounds of pursuit had her rising to her feet. The sudden fiery pain had her clenching her teeth to keep from crying out. Apparently the cloth had warmed some circulation back into her feet, making them throb far worse than before.

But that was nothing compared to what a bullet could do.

"I can make it," she announced, not entirely sure whether she could or not. But she had to try.

He gave her an approving look and took her hand, leading her through the dark, sure-footed as if he really did know the way by heart. Lightning still flashed, though less frequently now. But he didn't seem to need the bright light to guide him.

Careful to hold leaves and branches out of her way, he kept her close, guiding her footsteps. At first she thought he was being considerate, but as the sounds of pursuit faded, she realized everything he was doing was deliberate. He was helping her make as little noise as possible as they passed through the woods.

When her feet were throbbing so much she worried she couldn't take another step, he stopped.

"We're here," he whispered.

She wasn't sure where "here" was until lightning lit up the sky above them. They stood in front of a cluster of rocks that formed a small hill. But he led her around a large boulder and she saw what she hadn't seen before: the entrance to a cave.

He went in first, sweeping his gun out in front. What little light there was barely pierced the blackness of the cave. But the lightning filtered into the opening, showing it was empty.

She shivered at the thought of what could have been in there. Wild animals, she supposed. Probably nothing like a bear on a small island like this, but there could have been any number of smaller animals, all of them dangerous if cornered or if they carried rabies. She rubbed her hands up and down her arms. At least it wasn't raining here. That was something.

"You're cold." He shoved his gun in the holster on

his belt and started to unstrap his Kevlar vest as if to wrap it around her.

She placed her hand on his, stopping him. “No. That’s all you have to keep yourself warm. You already gave up your shirt for me. I’ll not have you freeze to death by giving me your vest.”

He dropped his hands to his sides and nodded. “At least it’s dry in here. I’d start a fire, but it would be a beacon to the gunmen. Come on. Sit and we’ll huddle together to get warm.”

The images *that* conjured in her mind had her feeling warm all over.

“I promise I’ll behave,” he added, as if he thought she might be worried about his intentions.

Ashley snorted. “Don’t expect me to make the same promise.”

He laughed. “I consider myself forewarned.”

She gave him an answering grin, felt her way to the far wall and slid to the ground. Thankfully it was dirt, not rock, making it a *little* less hard than the solid wall at their backs.

He sank down next to her, keeping his gun on his far side, sitting close but not touching. She let out an exasperated breath. She was freezing. Now wasn’t the time to worry that they were practically strangers. She scooted closer until his hard thigh pressed against hers. Not feeling nearly warm enough, she lifted his arm and pulled it around her shoulders.

He chuckled and pulled her closer. “Are you always this shy, or am I special for some reason?”

Oh, he was definitely special, but no way was she saying *that.*

“I wouldn’t normally snuggle up to a stranger, but

I'm cold and you're like a furnace. Impossible to resist at the moment."

He laughed again and rubbed his hand up and down her arm, warming her even more.

Wouldn't he be surprised if he knew how tempted she was to crawl onto his lap and wrap her arms around him, to get as close as possible and *really* get warm? That thought almost had her giggling, and that's when she realized how exhausted she must be. She was not a giggling kind of girl. And she certainly wasn't a crawl-into-the-lap-of-a-stranger kind of girl, either.

"Miss Parrish—Ashley, what happened back at your house?" He asked the question in a quiet, hushed voice, as if to make sure no one outside could hear him.

She yawned, covering her mouth with her hand.

"I was on the phone with my friend Lauren, and the phone went dead. The next thing I knew, Iceman ran down the hall and pointed a gun at me."

"Iceman?"

"The first guy, the one who drove the truck. He pulled me out of the house and made me get into his pickup. Somehow he'd managed to park out back without me knowing."

"And you call him Iceman because?"

She shuddered. "Because his eyes are like ice. Cold and dead."

He lightly squeezed her arm. "You didn't recognize him? Or the other man?"

"Baldy? No, I didn't recognize either of them. Honestly, I have no idea why people are suddenly trying to kill me. I'm a CPA, for goodness' sake. I inspire fear in no one."

"I disagree. You perform audits, right? That's why

you were at Gibson and Gibson. Most people are intimidated by auditors."

"If I worked for the IRS, I'd agree with you. But when I audit a company, it's usually because that company hired me. They need my reports to convince banks to give them loans, or to prove their practices are pursuant to regulations and tax laws."

"So there *are* times when you're hired by an outside company? And the company you audit isn't happy that you're there?"

"Well, I suppose that's one way to look at it. Yes."

"What happens to a company if your audit reveals problems? Worst case."

"Well, worst case, someone goes to jail. But I don't think that's ever happened in any companies I've worked with. I really don't have any way of knowing that for sure. I just provide the information and leave. I'm not the enemy."

"Has anyone ever lost a loan because of your findings? Or been fired?"

She shifted her weight against the hard ground and stifled a yawn. Dillon's heat was starting to make her drowsy.

"Ashley?"

She blinked and realized she'd started to nod off. "Sorry. What did you ask?"

"Whether companies lose loans or employees get fired when you find discrepancies."

She nodded. "Of course. There's always something at stake in an audit. And there are always consequences."

"Then it sounds to me like you *are* the enemy, at least sometimes, to some people."

She thought back over the many contracts she'd had in the six years that she'd been an auditor. "Honestly,

I couldn't say. When I turn in audit results, that's the end of my assignment. I don't even know what happens once I'm gone. I move to the next contract, the next client." She yawned again.

He pressed her head down onto his shoulder. "We can talk more later. Try to get some sleep. Sorry you have to sleep in a cave, but we should be safe here. I'll keep watch for Iceman and Baldy."

She heard the laughter in his voice, but his teasing reminder about keeping watch had her blinking her eyes and looking toward the cave entrance again. How could she have forgotten about Iceman out there searching for her? Supposedly he needed her alive, for whatever purpose he had in mind, but she wasn't so sure he was going to stick to that dictate now that she'd shot him in the shoulder.

"I'll help you keep watch," she whispered. "There's no way I can sleep knowing those men are looking for us. As for the accommodations, no worries. This won't be the first time I've slept in a cave."

"YOU'VE SLEPT IN a cave before?" Dillon was both surprised and curious to know what circumstances would make her *want* to sleep in a cave. When he'd seen her in a conservative gray skirt and matching suit jacket this morning, she hadn't struck him as the outdoors, camping type. And he'd noticed the reluctance in her eyes when she contemplated sitting on the rotten hull of a tree earlier so he could bandage her cuts. Getting dirty or risking a bug or two crawling on her would probably go in her auditor column of negatives instead of positives.

Apparently he'd have to wait for the answer to his question. Her breaths had grown deep and even. She'd already fallen asleep. He couldn't help but smile. She'd probably be horrified to realize she'd fallen asleep after declaring she would help him keep watch. Not that he wanted her help. Her bravery in the face of danger had already scared the hell out of him today. Twice.

Most women he knew—heck, most *men* he knew—wouldn't approach an armed man unless they were armed, too. Ashley had done that twice in one day, both times to try to help him. He hadn't needed her help, but she hadn't realized that. She thought he was in trouble and had jumped right in, with no thought for her own safety.

That kind of bravery was rare, but it was also dangerous. Sometimes jumping in to help someone wasn't the best option, and it was more likely to get them hurt, or killed. Hopefully she'd never have to learn that lesson the hard way.

Like he had.

He shied away from those thoughts. Those memories were better left buried and taken out when his only company was a bottle of Jack Daniel's.

He settled more comfortably against the hard rock wall, wishing the storm would hurry and break. His men were probably out in the rain right now looking for him since he hadn't checked back in after his last callout. Once they found his Jeep and saw the deep ruts the truck had left beside the river, they'd figure out at least part of what had happened. He just prayed they'd figure it out before the gunmen realized he and Ashley were holed up in this cave.

If he'd been stranded on Cooper's Bluff by himself, he wouldn't hide. He'd go on the offensive, sneak up behind his pursuers. But with an innocent civilian to worry about, that wasn't an option. If something happened to him, Ashley would be left alone to fend for herself. That wasn't a risk he was willing to take.

She whimpered and jerked against him in her sleep, and mumbled something that sounded like "Iceman." He rubbed his hand up and down her arm, trying to soothe her, but she continued to toss and turn. Feeling helpless and rusty in the ways of comforting a woman, he whispered nonsensical words to her, much like he did to his horses back home when they were agitated. To his chagrin, she immediately calmed down and relaxed against his side. He had a feeling if she ever found out he'd treated her like a horse, she wouldn't be a bit pleased.

Several hours later, the storm finally relinquished its hold on Cooper's Bluff. Thunder rumbled only occasionally now in the distance, and the flashes of lightning were replaced with the first rays of sunlight filtering into the cave. He could pick out details now, like Ashley's curly brown hair falling across her face as she lay against his chest. However, the arrival of dawn was not something to celebrate.

Because the blood drops from Ashley's wounds were now visible to their pursuers.

This was the moment he'd dreaded. It had been too dark last night to be sure he'd wrapped her feet well enough to prevent the blood trail from giving their location away. And although he didn't think he'd broken any branches and he'd kept them walking on hard ground as much as he could, it was impossible not to leave some evidence of their passing in the damp earth. Staying in the cave was no longer a safe option. They'd have to take their chances on the run again.

He gently shook her. "Ashley, wake up."

She mumbled in her sleep and lightly punched his arm. Apparently she wasn't a morning person.

He shook her again. “Wake up. We have to—”

A loose rock shifted at the entrance.

Dillon dove in front of Ashley as a gunman stepped into the cave.

Chapter Six

"Whoa, whoa, whoa." Chris Downing raised his hands in the air, his pistol pointing up toward the roof of the cave. "You aren't still mad about Becky Abrams, are you? That was twelfth grade, man."

Dillon lowered his gun. "For the record, Becky slept with you because she knew I wasn't interested."

"Ouch." Chris grinned and holstered his weapon. "Looks like you're in one piece, but your lady friend could use a doctor. What happened to her feet?"

Ashley had slumped over but was still sound asleep with her head pillowed on her arm. Dillon winced when he saw the bright red splotches on her bandages.

"I didn't realize the cuts were that bad. We had to run halfway across the island and she didn't have any shoes." He looked past Chris to the cave opening. "Did you come alone?"

"Randy and Max came with me, but they're following a trail some clueless city slickers made. Two sets of footprints slogging through mud, broken branches all over the place. Whoever left that trail must have run through the woods like a herd of cattle in a stampede."

"I don't think they were worried about leaving a trail.

Make sure Randy and Max know the men they're following are armed and extremely dangerous."

"We all kind of figured that when we found the truck tangled up in the downed tree with the passenger window shot out."

"When are they supposed to report in?"

He checked his watch. "About six more minutes."

Dillon debated whether to wait for their call or retrieve his men right now so he could get Ashley off the island. She needed those feet tended to, might even need stitches. But if the men who were after her got away, she would still be in danger if they decided to come after her again. And next time, she might not be lucky enough to have a friend call the police.

She mumbled in her sleep and shifted position.

"You going to tell me what happened?" Chris asked. "We know you responded to a nine-one-one call to check on Miss Parrish, but never called to make a report."

"You found my Jeep?"

He nodded. "After a search up and down Little River Road, we started searching side roads until we found your car. We found tire tracks by the river, along with your jacket. Since the river had rapids last night an Olympic white-water rafter wouldn't dare try, I'm pretty sure I have to be wrong about what it looks like you did. Because no one with any brains in his head would have gone for a swim in that river, not in that storm. That would have been a suicide mission."

"Apparently not, since I'm still here."

Chris cursed. "You, of all people, know how dangerous a rain-swollen river can—"

"Don't," Dillon rasped, his fists clenching at his sides. "Don't you dare go there."

They stood nose to nose, each of them staring the

other one down. Finally, Chris backed up and held his hands out in a placating gesture.

"Sorry," he mumbled.

Dillon let out the breath he didn't even realize he was holding. He gave Chris a curt nod and forced his fists to relax.

Chris held his hand out. Dillon clasped it and Chris hauled him to his feet.

"Why didn't you call for backup?" Chris asked.

"I couldn't. My cell phone wouldn't work. I'm pretty sure the man who drove that truck had a cell phone jammer."

"A cell phone jammer? Fill in the gaps, boss man," Chris insisted.

"When I got to Miss Parrish's house, a man took off with her in a truck. I followed them and tried to call for backup, but the call wouldn't go through. I figured the signal was jammed but I couldn't risk falling back far enough to get a clear signal. I would have lost them. I followed them to the bridge, where the fool driver ended up in the water."

"Who shot the window out?"

"I did. I tried to pull Miss Parrish out the window before the truck slid the rest of the way into the river."

Chris crossed his arms. "And you thought it was a good idea to jump in? The river was too rough last night for us to risk taking the boat out, but you went for a frickin' swim."

"I told you. I didn't have a choice."

Chris's answering frown told Dillon what his friend thought of that statement.

"Regardless, when I got on the island the man who'd abducted her was tying her up. I managed to handcuff one of his wrists when another man came out of the woods and got the drop on me. You pretty much know the rest. We ran and hid in the cave."

"Tell me about these guys."

"I can't say much for the second guy, didn't get a good look at him. But the first one, the one who abducted Miss Parrish, he was hardcore, stone-cold dangerous, focused on his mission."

"He must not have been too focused, since you two are still alive."

Dillon shook his head. "He wasn't trying to kill us, or at least, he wasn't trying to kill her. He could have done that back at her house. His goal last night was to kidnap her."

"Any clue why?"

"Not yet."

"I don't suppose it occurred to you it's a heck of a coincidence that Miss Parrish was involved in two different shootings in one day?"

"I've thought of little else since last night. There's got to be a connection. Either that or she's the world's most unlucky accountant ever."

"I'm hoping for bad luck, personally," a feminine voice interjected. "Seems to be the lesser of two evils."

Dillon and Chris turned to see Ashley sitting up, shoving her hair out of her face.

Chris stepped over to her and offered his hand. "I'm Chris, in case you forgot. We met at Gibson and Gibson yesterday morning."

"I remember. I'd say nice to see you again, but I'd be lying. No offense." She shook his hand.

He laughed. "None taken."

A sound near the entrance had Dillon standing protectively in front of Ashley while Chris drew his gun.

"Police," a voice called out. Seconds later, Max and Randy stepped into view.

Chris holstered his weapon.

"You didn't find them," Dillon said, disappointment heavy in his voice.

"No. Looks like they had a boat on the east side of the island at the community dock. They must have left some time during the night, or maybe early this morning before we got here. We didn't hear a boat motor."

Dillon introduced Max and Randy to Ashley. "Destiny's a pretty small town, so our police officers fill many roles. Max, Randy and Chris—like me—are detectives and SWAT, when needed. They were at the office shooting yesterday, too."

Ashley waved and offered a small smile.

Dillon noted the light flush of embarrassment on her face and the way her eyes slid longingly toward the entrance. He had a pretty good idea he knew why. "Where'd you moor the boat?" he asked Max, meaning the police boat.

"Back side of the island, about a hundred yards due west, by the old Cub Scout campground."

"You guys go ahead. Miss Parrish and I will catch up in a few minutes. I need to ask her a question."

The men filed out and Dillon squatted down beside Ashley. "Can you walk?"

She nodded and started to push herself up. But the moment she put her weight on her feet, she gasped and fell back.

Dillon caught her and scooped her up in his arms, cradling her against his chest. "That's what I thought. We'll get you to a doctor first thing." He carried her out of the cave and set her down on a boulder near some bushes.

She glanced up, her eyes questioning. "I thought we were going to a boat."

"I figured your bladder might be suffering the same as mine after spending the night sleeping in a cave. And I didn't think you'd want to bump around in a boat without taking a quick break first. These bushes should offer you some privacy."

Her face turned a light shade of pink. "You're right. Thank you."

He bent down at eye level with her. "Do you need me to hold you up? I promise I won't look."

She shook her head back and forth, her face turning a darker shade of red. "No, thank you. I'll manage, somehow. Just give me a few minutes. Please."

"All right. I won't be far. Call out if you need me." He watched her hobble over behind the bushes, her face a mask of pain every time she took a step. When he was satisfied she wasn't going to fall on her face, he hurried off to give her the promised privacy, and to answer nature's call himself.

A few minutes later, he found Ashley sitting back on the boulder, her face still flushed a delightful shade of pink.

"Ready?" he asked.

She nodded, and he scooped her up in his arms again.

When they reached the boat, Chris gave them a curious glance but didn't say anything. Dillon set Ashley in the forward seat on the port side, a few feet from Chris's position at the wheel, while he and Randy took up positions on the benches that ran along the port and starboard sides. Max untied the mooring line from the back of the boat and Chris eased it out into the river.

Noting Ashley's curious glance at the fishing poles lying in the middle bottom of the boat, Dillon explained,

"Destiny's residents don't figure their tiny police force needs a fancy speedboat like some of the bigger cities have. This old fishing boat might not be fast or fancy, but it's sturdy, and generally suits our needs."

"Understandable, but why the fishing poles?"

Chris half turned and grinned. "Those are mine. I like to be prepared for emergencies."

"Is there such thing as a fishing emergency?"

"Of course. You never know when the fish will be biting." He turned the boat upriver, the glassy, smooth surface nothing like the roiling, raging death trap from last night.

"I can see that accountant's mind whirling now," Dillon teased. "You're wondering if Chris compensates the department for use of the boat, and the fuel."

"I was doing nothing of the sort."

"Sure you were."

She narrowed her eyes and turned to face the front as Chris steered the boat around a curve in the river.

Damage from the storm was far worse than Dillon had expected. White birch and oak trees had given up their fight and lay on their sides in several areas along the bank, broken branches trailing in the water, causing little eddies as the current swirled around them.

The guttural sound of a powerful engine roaring to life had Dillon whirling around.

"Look out," Ashley shouted. She lunged toward Chris and knocked him to the floor of the boat just as a shot rang out. The windshield in front of the pilot's chair exploded into a spiderweb, right where Chris's head had been seconds ago.

He blinked in shock at Ashley.

"Keep her down," Dillon ordered. Chris immediately covered Ashley with his body.

Dillon fired three quick shots at the gunman aiming at them from the speedboat on the other side of the river. It was coming up fast, directly toward them. Baldy was at the wheel. Iceman was beside him, taking potshots at the police boat.

"Grab the wheel, Randy," Dillon ordered as he and Max fired several more shots at the speedboat.

Randy ducked down and made his way around Chris and Ashley to steer the boat.

The speedboat accelerated.

Dillon cursed. "Make this thing move! Max, lay down cover fire. I'm going to try to pick off Baldy."

Max pulled the trigger, but the gun was empty. He tossed it to the floor. "Chris, gun!"

Chris tossed his pistol to Max, who caught it and whirled back around, shooting round after round.

Iceman dove to the floor of the speedboat, leaving the driver vulnerable.

"Who's Baldy?" Max yelled.

Dillon steadied his gun and took one very careful shot. *Boom!*

"He's history," Dillon gritted out.

Baldy slumped over the wheel and the speedboat turned hard to the port side, spinning out of control without someone to steer it. His body slid off the seat and the engine choked, then stopped. The boat bounced on its own wake and started drifting on the current.

"Cease fire," Dillon ordered. "Randy, bring the boat around. Max, stay alert."

Max stayed on his knees, aiming his gun toward the side of the speedboat, waiting for the other shooter to emerge again.

Dillon glanced at Chris, still covering Ashley. "Both of you okay?"

Ashley's wide-eyed gaze peeked out from beneath Chris's shoulder. She gave Dillon a tentative nod.

"Thanks to Miss Parrish, I didn't get my head blown off," Chris responded, his voice sounding raw.

Dillon tightened his hold on his gun and focused on the speedboat. Randy shut off the engine and let the fishing boat drift up to the side.

Max and Dillon aimed their guns into the floor of the boat.

Empty.

They glanced at each other in surprise, then both jumped into the boat.

"Where the heck did he go?" Max asked. He hurried over to the driver's body and felt his neck for a pulse, then shook his head.

Dillon stared out over the smooth, dark surface of the river. "My guess, he went into the water and swam to shore." He looked back at the police boat, a slow, lumbering beast. "Start making calls. Get the state police to put a chopper in the air and get another boat out here. Make sure they know a shooter might be in the woods. They'll need to stop short of this location and hike the rest of the way in. Have the Blount County coroner meet me at Cooper's Bluff Bridge, or what's left of it. And get a BOLO out on our missing shooter."

He gave Max a quick, detailed description for the be-on-the-lookout announcement that would go out to every law enforcement agency in the county, from Cades Cove to Rockford, as well as neighboring counties. "Max, put a personal call out to Chief Massey at Bitterwood P.D. over in Ridge County, too. Bitterwood's small enough and close enough to appeal to a gunman on foot trying to evade police."

Max nodded and grabbed his cell phone.

Dillon hopped back into the police boat. "I've got her now," he told Chris.

As soon as Chris moved out of the way, Dillon scooped Ashley up again and hurried with her to the speedboat. He set her on the floor. "Lie down. Don't sit up. Iceman's still out there."

She didn't answer. She was too busy staring at Baldy lying lifeless a few feet away.

"Don't look at him. Close your eyes."

She squeezed her eyes shut.

"Chris, get over here. You're coming with us," Dillon called out.

Chris was standing with Randy at the wheel of the police boat. He gave Randy a puzzled look then hurried to the speedboat and got in.

"What are you doing?" Chris asked.

"Getting the shooter's main target out of here. Once we get back to the bridge to Cooper's Bluff, you'll need to stay with the boat to wait for the coroner to pick up our dead friend here. I'll drive Miss Parrish back to town to get her medical attention."

Max put his cell phone away. "State police are on the way. And Chief Massey offered to send reinforcements if you need them."

"Good to know. Thanks, Max. Get back on the other boat. You guys get to shore and hunker down in the woods until the state police get here. If our guy's got some dry weapons stashed nearby, he'll start taking shots again. I don't want you in the middle of the river when he does."

Max frowned with obvious disappointment. "We don't need to wait. If the shooter's in those woods, Randy and I can find him."

"Wait for backup. That's an order."

Max gave him a curt nod and joined Randy.

Dillon restarted the engine, and turned the speedboat back toward the bridge.

WHEN DILLON CARRIED Ashley into the one-story offices of the Destiny Police Department, it only took a quick turn of her head to get the layout of the entire police station. One unisex bathroom to her left. Fifteen cheap laminate desks lined up in three rows in the middle of the rectangular room. A snack machine and tiny kitchenette on the right beside a door labeled Chief of Police, William Thornton. And along the back wall, two currently unoccupied cells with floor-to-ceiling iron bars.

Take away the computers and phones, sprinkle in a few cowboy hats, and the place could be the setting of an old TV Western.

"I'm sure I can walk," she whispered, feeling silly in his arms as he strode past the handful of police officers working at their desks.

"Doesn't mean you should." When he reached the first jail cell, he hooked one of the nearby desk chairs with his foot and dragged it over, then carefully set Ashley on the chair. "Give me a sec."

He crossed to a small cabinet built into the wall and unlocked it, then pulled out a big brass key.

Ashley watched in stunned amazement as he used the key to unlock the first cell and swung the door open.

He caught her watching him and raised a brow. "What?"

"You do realize what century we're in, right? You don't have electronic locks on the cells?"

He smiled and tossed the key in the air, easily catching it. "The city council wouldn't approve more than a cheap, used fishing boat for the police department. Do you really think they'd approve an expensive electronic locking system for our jail?"

She shrugged and eyed the cell. "Please tell me you're not thinking about locking me in there."

"You need to be protected. Makes sense to lock you up, don't you think?"

"I'm going home." She shot up out of her chair but immediately fell back to sitting when pain shot through her feet.

Dillon crouched down in front of her and took her hand in his. "That was a really bad joke. I promise I'm not going to lock you up. However, the cot in the cell is the most comfortable place with your feet the way they are. I figured you could lie down and elevate your feet while I call Doc Brookes. He still makes house calls and the nearest hospital is a long drive from here."

She bit her lip in indecision. "Promise you won't lock the door?"

He crossed his heart. "Scout's honor."

"All right then. Putting my feet up does sound good. I guess you get to carry me one more time."

He squeezed her hand and let go. "Trust me. Carrying you is not a burden."

He scooped her up before she could think too hard about that comment. She couldn't imagine he'd meant it the way it sounded, as if he was flirting with her. Because after being in a rainstorm, spending all night in a cave and wearing the same muddy, dirty clothes without being able to even wash her face, there was nothing about her that could be even remotely attractive.

He propped her feet up on a pillow and pulled a blanket over her. "I'll be right back."

"Wait, please. Do you have a phone I can use? You said Lauren called nine-one-one last night because she was worried about me. I need to let her know I'm okay. Preferably before she calls my family and gets them worried and they descend en masse on Destiny and get all in my business."

He grinned. "Big, nosy family, huh?"

"Like you wouldn't believe."

"My phone is at the bottom of the river somewhere, but I'll get you one. Give me a minute."

While he headed over to a young policewoman sitting at a desk by the window, Ashley self-consciously finger combed her hair. Dillon perched on the edge of the desk and several officers came over to talk to him. Even without a shirt, wearing nothing but his bullet-resistant vest, wrinkled dress pants and boots, he still looked amazing. Ashley was suddenly longing for a hot shower, some fresh clothes and her makeup bag.

If Lauren could see her now, she'd accuse Ashley of being in lust with Dillon, and she would probably be right. She had a lot of other things she should be worrying about instead of drooling over the tall, dark and handsome man who'd been a part of her life for less than twenty-four hours. In all likelihood, once her feet were finally taken care of, he'd probably take her statement and send her on her way. She'd likely never see him again, unless he caught a suspect and needed her to testify or something. One thing was for sure, as soon as she could she was leaving Destiny way behind in her rearview mirror, never to pass this way again.

No matter how sexy Detective Dillon Gray was.

Dillon brought a cell phone and let Ashley make a quick call, reassuring her friend everything was okay. As usual, Lauren's melodramatic streak made the call take much longer than Ashley wanted, particularly when Dillon was waiting. But at least Lauren hadn't called her family yet, and Ashley was again able to talk her out of cutting her cruise short. She hung up and gave the phone back to Dillon.

"Thank you."

"Disaster averted?" he teased.

"Just barely."

He motioned back toward the squad room. The policewoman he'd spoken to earlier headed over. At the same time, the main door opened on the far end of the room and Detective Chris Downing stepped inside.

"Ashley Parrish," Dillon said when the policewoman stepped into the cell, "this is Officer Donna Waters."

"Pleasure," Donna said, shaking Ashley's hand.

"Donna's going to go to your house and pack you a bag so you can change into fresh clothes. I'll leave you two here to discuss what you need. I'm still trying to locate Doc Brookes."

He headed back to one of the desks and grabbed the phone. Chris stopped beside him and spoke to him while Dillon dialed the number.

"So," Donna said, drawing Ashley's attention to her. "Looks like you're going to be our prisoner until we catch whoever's after you."

Ashley blinked in surprise. "Dillon… I mean, Detective Gray said he wasn't going to lock me up in here. Scout's honor."

Donna burst out laughing. "Dillon was never a scout. Trust me on that. Honestly, I assumed he was going to keep you here for your own protection. Maybe he's got other plans." She pulled a small notebook and pen from her front shirt pocket. "Now, tell me exactly what you want from your house and I'll be happy to get it. I've already got the address. Since I don't see a purse with you, I'm assuming you don't have your keys. Is there a spare somewhere?"

"My landlord has a key. He lives a few miles down from my house, Mr. Hartley."

"I know him. No problem. I'll stop there first. Now, worst case, assuming you may not be able to go home for a few days, what all do you need?"

DILLON HUNG UP the phone and shot Chris an irritated glance. "Doc Brookes isn't answering his cell. His assistant said he's probably out of range, up in the foothills seeing some patient. And from what Donna told me a few minutes ago, there are trees and power lines down all over Destiny. It'll take hours to get her to a hospital."

Chris grinned. "No reason she should wait." He clapped Dillon on the shoulder. "Not when we've got our own doctor." He headed toward the cell.

"Chris, get your butt back here," Dillon ordered, but Chris ignored him and hurried into the cell.

Dillon chased after him, hoping to head off a disaster.

"Miss Parrish, good to see you again," Chris said. "Looks like with the storm and all, we're down to only one doctor anywhere nearby who can take care of you."

Dillon strode into the cell and aimed a murderous glare at Chris.

"And here he is," Chris announced, waving toward Dillon.

Donna coughed as if she was trying not to laugh.

Ashley stared up at Dillon, her eyes wide with surprise. "You're a doctor?"

"No," Dillon said.

"Yes," Donna and Chris both said at the same time.

"Knock it off," Dillon ordered. "Miss Parrish, I did go to medical school, but not the kind of—"

"I'll get your bag," Chris announced. "I assume it's in the Jeep? You never go anywhere without it." He hurried out of the cell, steering well clear of Dillon's reach.

"Now everything makes sense," Ashley said. "You seemed to know what you were doing when you wrapped my cuts last night."

He closed his eyes and prayed for patience.

Donna laughed. "He's definitely good at doctoring. Did his schooling in Nashville."

He opened his eyes again and glared at her, not that it did any good.

"Really?" Ashley asked. "That's where I'm from. Did you go to TSU? I graduated from there."

"As a matter of fact, yes, I went to Tennessee State University. I'm trying to explain that I'm not—"

"He graduated with honors," Donna chimed in again.

"Here we go." Chris ran into the cell carrying a small black duffel bag. He set it beside the cot. "Go ahead, Dr. Gray. Fix her feet."

Dillon pointed to the cell door. "Out. Both of you. Now."

Donna patted Ashley's hand. "Don't you worry. I'll get what you need and be back in no time."

She and Chris hurried out of the cell, apparently deciding retreat was a good idea.

Dillon glared after them, then dragged the chair from outside the cell and settled it in front of the cot. He plopped down and tried to tamp down his anger before saying anything. Ashley looked completely confused, not that he could blame her.

"Detective—"

"Dillon."

"Right, sorry. What was all that about? What's going on? Are you really a doctor?"

He shook his head. "No, I'm not. That was Chris and Donna's idea of a joke. Unfortunately, Chris was right about one thing. There's no one around who can take care of you right now. I'm going to have to drive you to Blount Memorial in Maryville. Normally that would be a forty-minute drive, but with the storm damage, it's going to probably take closer to three hours. Do you want to leave now, or wait for Donna to get back with fresh clothes? There's a shower in the bathroom in the chief's office. I'm sure he wouldn't mind—"

She put her hand on his. Awareness shot through him, surprising him. He glanced up at her.

"Dillon," she said. "My feet hurt. A lot. If there's something you can do to help me, I'd really appreciate it. I don't relish the idea of driving for three hours with my feet throbbing if you can make me feel better right now. What were your friends teasing about, exactly? Did you not really graduate? Did you drop out early from TSU?"

He shook his head. "No. I graduated. But I did drop out of the University of Tennessee. I went there for my postgraduate studies."

A look of relief flashed across her face. "I don't care if you ended up with an official piece of paper or not. You had four years plus of training. Surely you can handle a few stitches and some fresh bandages. What's in the bag? I hope you have something stronger than Advil in there." She reached down and grabbed the bag.

Dillon rose out of his chair to stop her, but she'd already unzipped the bag before he could. Her eyes widened in horror.

"You're a veterinarian?"

Somewhere out in the squad room, Chris howled with laughter.

Dillon dropped his forehead in his hands and prayed

for patience. The sound of feminine laughter had him jerking his head back up.

Ashley's eyes danced with amusement. "Oh, come on. I figured out you studied veterinary medicine the minute Chris ran in here with that bag and made such a show out of calling you *doctor.* Plus, I went to TSU. I'm well aware they have a veterinary premed program there."

He shook his head. "You could have clued me in earlier."

"I was having too much fun. So what do you do, carry your bag around to take care of stray dogs and cats?"

"More like horses."

Her brows rose. "Horses. Cool." She looked in the bag. "Looks to me like you've got everything you could possibly need to sew a few stitches and bandage me up. I refuse to take any horse tranquilizers, so you're going to have to give me some of the strongest human medicine you can find in this office, or find a bottle of whiskey so I can get drunk first."

He dragged the bag toward him and pulled out a small jar. "If you don't mind the smell, I promise this numbing cream will work wonders. You won't feel a thing while I stitch you up."

"It can't smell worse than I probably already smell right now. Let's do this."

DAMN BLOODHOUNDS.

Luther would have been fine if it wasn't for the stupid dogs. He could have lain low in the woods until the local yokels gave up looking for him. Then he would have tracked down that detective to find out where he'd taken Parrish. But someone had called the state police to join the search, and sent in tracking dogs—probably the same nosy detective. Now he was forced to hightail it out of town in one of the cars he'd stashed for just such an emergency, which meant it would take that much longer to get the job done and put Hicktown, Tennessee, in his rearview mirror.

He checked the mirror again to make sure no one was following him before using the burn phone from the emergency bag he'd stowed in the car. Because of his hurt shoulder he had to keep the phone on the seat and use the speaker function. It was the only way he could drive and still punch the buttons, since he couldn't lift his right arm without it hurting like the dickens.

Ashley Parrish was going to pay for that, dearly.

"It's me," he said as soon as the phone clicked. "Johnson's dead, and the state police are looking for me. I've got to lie low for a few hours outside of town."

"Lie low? No, you can't. You have to do this *now.*"

He tightened his fingers on the phone. Very few people talked to him that way and lived to tell about it. If she were anyone else, he'd cut her tongue out for that. "If I go back right now, this whole thing is over. We both lose everything. Is that what you want?"

"No, no, of course not. I'm just anxious, worried. We don't have much time. I'm…sorry."

It probably killed her to say that. He couldn't help but grin.

"This is a minor blip in our plans. By this time tomorrow, I'll have Ashley Parrish exactly where we want her." He slowed and turned down the gravel road he'd been searching for. The bumpy ride sent a sharp pain shooting through his shoulder. He drew a sharp breath, then slowly let it out. "I've got to go."

"Call me as soon as you have her." She hung up without waiting for him to respond.

He squeezed the steering wheel so hard it bit into his palm. He'd had about all he could take of her orders and her lack of respect. Once he had his money, maybe he'd take the time to teach her a valuable lesson in how to deal with men like him.

He glanced in the rearview mirror again. But this time he didn't look at the road behind him. He looked at his guest sitting gagged and tied up in the backseat, staring at him with wide, fear-filled eyes—Dr. Brookes.

Chapter Seven

Showering in the police chief's executive bathroom had been an incredibly awkward experience. Dillon had wrapped Ashley's feet in plastic garbage bags to keep the bandages dry. Then he'd dragged in two chairs, one for her to sit on and one for her to prop her feet on, which made washing herself a difficult and time-consuming process. But all the trouble had been worth it to finally feel clean again.

Now, sitting with Dillon, Chris and Chief Thornton in the chief's office, which apparently doubled as a conference room, she felt awkward and sloppy dressed in loose sweats. The clothes were a present her mother had sent last week for her twenty-eighth birthday. She'd never worn them before, had never planned on wearing them, but she'd asked Donna to grab them in case she couldn't pull on any of her slacks over the bandages. Sure enough, they'd been the only clothes she could get on and she was grateful to have them. She'd have to remember to tell her mother later—much later, when it was too late to worry—that the sweats had turned out to be the best present she'd ever given her.

Now if only her mother had sent her some granola bars with those sweats, she'd be warm, comfy and her stomach wouldn't be eating a hole through her spine right now. It was getting close to noon and she'd yet to eat anything. That hadn't mattered until all her other aches and pains went away. Suddenly, it was almost all she could focus on—how hungry she was. If only she could be back home right now, cooking up one of her infamous breakfasts, the kind her brothers used to brag to all their friends about. Cooking was one of the few family traditions she'd actually appreciated.

"Miss Parrish?"

Ashley looked up at the police chief, chagrined to realize he must have been talking to her while she was fantasizing about eggs, bacon and waffles.

"Yes, sir?"

His eyes crinkled at the corners, reminding her of her father and how his smile always reached his eyes. She'd gotten the impression Dillon didn't care too much for his superior, but she'd found him nothing but charming.

"You must be tired and hungry," he said. "And we're obviously boring you with all this talk about the investigations. Detective Gray has volunteered to put you up at his house until we catch the man who abducted you and can ensure it's safe for you to go back home."

Ashley straightened in her chair. From the stony look on Dillon's face, she gathered *volunteered* might not have been the right description. What all had she missed while she'd daydreamed about comfy clothes and hot breakfast?

"Chief, I think there's been a misunderstanding," she said. "I don't live in Destiny. I'm only renting while on assignment here. My lease is up in two days— No, it's up tomorrow, actually. I don't need to impose on Detective Gray or anyone else. I'd appreciate an escort back to my house to get the rest of my things, but other than that, all I have to do is jump in my car and go back to my apartment in Nashville."

"How are you going to drive?" Dillon asked. "Or walk?"

Her face flushed hot remembering the house slippers she'd been forced to wear, since her feet were too swollen to fit in her shoes. Dillon had managed to wash up somewhere and was wearing one of his perfectly pressed suits again, looking ridiculously handsome and rested. And the other detectives—Chris, Max, Randy—had managed to bathe and change, as well. Looking at them reminded her how poor a condition she was in. Driving was the least of her worries. Dillon was right about that.

"I hadn't thought about the driving part. I'll get a cab to take me to the airport. I can come back for my car later."

"The nearest airport is in Knoxville," Chris piped in. "You're going to take a cab all the way from Destiny to Knoxville?"

She fisted her hands beneath the table. "I didn't say I had it all figured out yet. I'm saying, there's no reason for me to stay here. I don't *want* to stay here."

Dillon rested his forearms on his knees. "I know you're anxious to get out of this town, and I certainly can't blame you after everything that's happened. But I don't think you've really thought this through. Three different people have tried to kill or abduct you in the past twenty-four hours. They've gone to a lot of trouble, risk and expense to do so. What makes you think whoever's behind this isn't going to send their thugs to Nashville if you leave?"

She swallowed, hard. "Honestly, I hadn't really considered that possibility."

"You can go to Nashville if you choose," the chief

interjected. "We certainly can't stop you, and I'd have one of my officers escort you there to ensure you didn't encounter any problems—not to mention saving you an enormous cab fee. But I agree with Detective Gray. The odds point to one person, a powerful person, being behind all of this. I don't think they're going to stop just because you go home. Do you have family in Nashville that might be in danger if you go back?"

"Uh, no. Actually, my family is from…somewhere else."

"A boyfriend, coworkers, friends?" the chief continued.

Her gaze slid to Dillon. "No boyfriend, but of course I have people I care about back home. You don't really think they'd be in danger, do you? If I go back?"

"They might be, yes. One of the advantages of a small town like Destiny is that everyone knows everyone's business. I believe you're much safer here, with Detective Gray watching out for you, than you'd be at home. And having you here to answer questions and help with the ongoing investigations is quite helpful to us. We'd appreciate it if you'd at least consider staying for a couple of days."

She chewed her bottom lip. "Are the state police still searching for Iceman?"

His brow furrowed. "Iceman?"

"That's what she calls the shooter," Dillon said.

The chief smiled. "Okay, then no, they haven't found him. They're still looking, and two of my best trackers are with them. We will find him, eventually. But it's going to take some time. Meanwhile, I'd feel a lot better knowing you're safely tucked away with one of my best officers watching over you."

Dillon shot the chief a surprised look, as if he hadn't realized the chief considered him to be one of his best officers.

With the chief, Dillon and Chris watching her and waiting for her answer, all her arguments suddenly seemed foolish, and selfish. Stanley Gibson and seven others had died yesterday. If they'd died because someone was after her, then she owed it to them, to their families, to help find their killer in any way that she could.

"All right. I'll stay."

THE SUN WAS high in the sky announcing the noon hour by the time Dillon turned his Jeep down a long, dusty dirt road. Ashley was surprised that wherever he lived wasn't back in town. She'd expected him to want to live closer to the police station. Then again, as small as Destiny was, maybe close was all relative.

She heard the buzz of his cell phone and he reached down and pressed a button without even looking at it.

"Don't you need to see who's trying to call you?" she asked.

"It's the security system at my house. The motion sensors were triggered by my Jeep turning onto the access road. It automatically texts me to let me know I've got company coming. It even sends me a picture." He pulled the phone out and held it up.

The screen showed a strikingly clear picture of his Jeep with him at the wheel and her sitting beside him.

"Impressive," she said.

"Not half as impressive as all the pictures of stray cows I've been texted when they break out of my neighbor's fence and wander onto my property." He grinned. "But thankfully the sensor isn't set to trigger for anything much smaller than that. There are perimeter cameras on the property, too, overkill way out here. But security tends to be on my mind in my line of work. And I'd rather be too careful than careless."

She nodded, agreeing wholeheartedly.

When the Jeep topped the final hill and Dillon's home came into view, Ashley's mouth dropped open. On one side, acres and acres of rolling green grass spread out as far as she could see, dotted with small groups of horses grazing with the backdrop of the Smoky Mountains behind them. On the other side, eight-foot-tall stalks of bone-dry field corn, ready for harvest, marched in rows up and over a hill. All of it was bordered by pristine white wood fences. And smack-dab in the middle, at the end of the road, was a collection of whitewashed clapboard buildings set back behind a two-story, lovingly preserved farmhouse.

"Careful, you'll catch a fly," Dillon teased.

"That gorgeous house, this land, those *horses,* they're all yours?"

"Passed down from my father's grandfather's grandfather, through six generations of Grays. Dad didn't want to deal with the upkeep so he gave it to me. He and Mom moved to a smaller farm not too far from here." His pride and love for his legacy was evident in his tone and in the way his eyes lit up.

He parked the Jeep beside the house and hopped out. He rounded the car with her duffel bag hanging off his shoulder, opened the door and scooped her into his arms. Him picking her up was becoming a routine she could easily grow accustomed to. But now especially, without the vest and only a dress shirt separating the two of them, it was absolute heaven being cradled against him, feeling his warmth, being able to wrap her arms around his neck.

Since he was staring down at her, probably wondering why she was staring up at him, she rushed to fill the silence. “How many horses are there?”

“Thirty-two. I never planned to have that many. Started with Boomerang and three mares. Naturally, there’ve been some foals born out of that. But mostly, Harmony Haven is a rescue farm.”

“Boomerang?”

“A stallion. He’s whistle trained. He can be galloping away as fast as he can go and if I whistle he turns around and comes right back, like a boomerang.”

She smiled. “You said this place is a rescue farm?”

“We take in horses that are abused or from people who can’t afford them anymore. Our adoption rate is about sixty percent once we rehabilitate the animals. But some have been too traumatized or are too scarred up for anyone to want them. Those are our permanent residents.” He jogged up the wide front steps to the wraparound porch.

“You keep saying ‘we’ and ‘our.’ Does someone else live here, too? Someone else in your family?” She glanced at the large glass oval in the front door as he twisted the knob, and wondered who else she was about to meet.

“I live in the house alone, but my farm manager and half a dozen farmhands live in the bunkhouse out back. Don’t worry. You’ll have plenty of privacy. They don’t come up to the house much. As I said, my mom and dad live up the road, about half an hour from here. But they’re out of state right now, visiting my brother in Montana.”

He carried her in, dropped the duffel bag on the floor

and set her on a soft sage-green couch. The floors were a rustic oak and the staircase in the back of the room was framed with a polished oak handrail and bright white wooden spindles. The main room was expansive, but the enormous burgundy throw rug in the middle of the room softened the space and helped make it homey.

"The master suite is on the bottom floor, that door behind you," he said, pointing over her shoulder. "I'll change the sheets and move some of my things to one of the rooms upstairs. It will be much easier for you to hobble around on the bottom floor. It's got its own bathroom, so that will make it easier, too."

"I hate for you to give up your room for me, but I really appreciate it. I'm not sure I could handle stairs right now."

"Are you—"

Her stomach chose that moment to rumble. Loudly. Her face flushed hot.

His lips curved up in a sensual smile that was like a punch in the gut. Good grief, the man was sexy.

"I was about to ask if you were hungry," he teased. "But I think I have my answer. I've been cooking for myself for over twelve years now, since the day I left for college. So I reckon I can rustle up something decent to eat. What are you in the mood for?"

"Anything that won't run away when I stick my fork in it."

He laughed. "That hungry, huh? You should have said something earlier. We could have grabbed food back in town. Soup and sandwiches are quick so you don't have to wait long. Sound okay?"

"Sounds wonderful. Thanks."

He grabbed the duffel and stood. "Chris mentioned he might stop by in a bit to brainstorm on the investigation.

I usually leave the door unlocked, but with everything that's happened, I'm keeping the house sealed up tight. If you see him at the front door, holler at him to use his key."

"Okay."

He grabbed a remote control off the thick oak coffee table and set it beside her. "If you want to watch TV, click that top button. The TV will pop up out of the table behind the other couch."

"Hmm. Sounds like a fancy luxury to have."

He gave her a droll look. "Electronic equipment isn't a luxury. It's a necessity. Especially during football season."

She rolled her eyes and he grinned again. Thankfully he headed to the bedroom to drop off her duffel bag before he could realize she was debating the merits of grabbing him and pulling him onto the couch with her. A girl could only take so many heart-melting smiles in twenty-four hours without suffering some kind of lust-crazed breakdown.

He headed back through the family room to what she supposed was the kitchen. But she carefully kept her gaze on his eyes this time instead of that devastating smile.

DILLON REACHED THE kitchen and sank into one of the chairs at the table in the middle of the room. He had to take a minute, just one, before making lunch. If Ashley smiled at him one more time he didn't know what was going to happen. Ever since she'd showered and came out in those sweatpants that molded to the contours of her perfect bottom, he'd been useless as a detective. All he could think about was pulling her onto his lap and kissing her until she begged him to take her to bed.

He drew a shaky breath, trying to focus on something else, anything else but the far-too-appealing woman in the other room. Thornton hadn't understood his reluctance to keep Ashley at his house. After all, any time some hotshot law-enforcement official or even a witness in a case needed somewhere to hole up, Dillon always offered his house. The only hotel in town was a disaster. And Dillon's farmhouse was huge, only twenty minutes outside of town, and his security cameras would pick up on any vehicles coming down the road long before they reached the house. But he'd known having Ashley here would kill his concentration. Unfortunately, he hadn't wanted to admit that to Thornton, so he'd grudgingly agreed to bring her home.

After another deep breath, he shoved out of the chair to fix the sexy little distraction something to eat. After that he'd call down to the office in the bunkhouse and make sure Griffin and his men knew to be on the lookout for anything suspicious. Iceman didn't strike Dillon as the kind of man to give up. And if he figured out Ashley was here, a few security cameras weren't going to stop him from going after his target again.

ASHLEY BLINKED AND opened her eyes. It took a moment to get her bearings. She was lying on the couch in Dillon's family room, a royal-blue quilt tucked around her and a soft pillow cushioning her head. The sun was fading from the large bank of windows out front and the glass oval in the door was turning black as the sun began to set. The last thing she remembered was thanking Dillon for the ham-and-cheese sandwich and vegetable soup. She must have fallen asleep and slept right through the dinner hour.

Deep voices carried to her from the back of the house

somewhere. She recognized Dillon's voice, and realized the other voice must be Chris. She must have been exhausted to sleep through his arrival.

She sat up and twisted around. The door to the bedroom wasn't that far away, and Dillon had mentioned there was a connected bathroom, a facility she was sorely in need of at the moment. Calling out to him to carry her to the bathroom was an embarrassment she didn't relish, especially if Chris was here, too. Surely she could hobble by herself without his help.

By using the arm of the couch, and then the back of the couch for support, she slowly, painfully made her way upright. Her feet were tender, bruised, but the fiery burn was gone. The salve Dillon had put on her cuts had already made a huge difference.

It took far longer than her bladder wanted, but she made it into the bathroom all by herself. She fist pumped the air, ridiculously happy to not be an invalid anymore, and quickly took care of her needs. She hobbled to the duffel bag on the bed and riffled through it. Sure enough, Donna had gotten everything on her list—clothes, makeup and even her laptop. Ashley grabbed a hairbrush and some makeup and made a mental note to find a way to express her appreciation to Donna and the men who'd risked their lives yesterday to save her, both at the office building and later on Cooper's Bluff.

A few minutes later, with her hair brushed and some makeup on her face, she felt like a brand-new woman. She slung the strap of her laptop case over her head, letting it hang across her shoulder. Then she cautiously made her way down the hallway she'd spotted underneath the staircase earlier.

Following the voices, she ended up in the doorway of a massive room in the back right corner of the house.

Floor-to-ceiling bookshelves lined two of the walls. The third wall had a bank of small TV screens, which she realized showed pictures of the road out front and various other angles of the farm—probably that fancy security system Dillon had told her about. The last wall was a bank of windows with an incredible view of the sun sinking over the mountains. Little puffs of white mist rose into the air all across those mountains. She remembered staring at that same mist as a little girl, asking her daddy if the mountains were on fire. He'd laughed and told her no, the mist was a natural phenomenon because of the climate, and the reason people called the mountains the Smokies.

"Well, hello," a male voice called out.

She tore her gaze from the picturesque view out the windows. Apparently Chris was the one who'd spoken, because he gave her a friendly wave. The two men sitting on either side of him around an enormous cherrywood table in the middle of the room smiled at her, as well. They were the SWAT officers who'd been with Dillon and Chris yesterday, the same ones who'd rescued them on the island—Max and Randy.

She returned Chris's wave and hobbled into the room. "Where's Dillon?" she asked.

"Right behind you."

She whirled around in surprise at the deep voice that sounded so close. The movement sent a sharp, fiery spike of pain up her calves and she started to fall.

"Whoa, whoa, I've got you." He caught her in his arms and lifted her against his chest. "You okay? Did you need something?"

"I, uh, no. I don't need anything. And you certainly don't need to carry me again."

"I don't mind." He winked.

Her face flushed hot. "I woke up and thought I'd do a little work." She patted her laptop bag. "I heard voices and followed them back here."

His gaze traveled over her hair and her face in a soft caress. "Looks like you might have made it into the bedroom, too, and did a little primping," he teased, his voice a whisper only she could hear. "For the record, you were already beautiful. But you look even better now."

She blinked, not sure what to say.

"So what's the verdict? Now that you know all us guys are here, do you want to stay or go back to the family room? We're reviewing the case files and brainstorming."

"I'd rather stay, if you don't mind. I won't get in the way. And if you have any questions for me, I'll be right here."

"Works for me." He strode to the table and gently set her on one of the padded chairs, then sat next to her.

She set her laptop on the table and turned it on. But the silence had her glancing back up. Three pairs of eyes were watching her. The only one who wasn't watching her was Dillon, who was silently reading from one of many folders scattered across the tabletop.

"Um, hi," she said. "Don't mind me. I need to finish my report for Mr. Gibson's bank. I'll sit here quietly."

Chris slid a bowl of pretzels across the table to her. "Hungry?"

"I could eat. Thanks." She popped a pretzel in her mouth.

"You'll need a drink," Max said. He appeared to be the youngest of them, probably fresh out of school. His angular face and dark hair made her wonder if he might have some Cherokee in him. "Water? Sweet tea? Beer?" he asked.

"Seriously, no one needs to wait on me. I'm fine."

Dillon looked up and frowned as if just realizing his men were staring at her. "We have work to do, guys. Max, you can grab her a drink, then hurry and get back in here."

Max eagerly nodded and headed out of the room.

For the first time since she'd met him, Ashley realized Dillon seemed aggravated. He must be irritated that she'd interfered with their work. She gave him an uncertain smile and focused on her computer screen, determined not to interfere anymore.

When Max returned with a glass of water, she thanked him. He nodded and gave her a shy smile before returning to his seat. The conversation started up around her again and she tuned it out so she could concentrate on typing the final conclusions into her report. It didn't take long, since she'd been mostly finished with it.

Using the Wi-Fi hotspot feature on her computer to access the internet, she emailed the report to the bank, with a copy to Ron Gibson. The poor man was probably grieving over the loss of his son and didn't care about the report right now, but he would later. And when he did, he'd be pleased to know she'd concluded his company was sound with no obvious causes for concern. He'd be able to get that bank loan if he still wanted it. She sent another email to Lauren, letting her know she'd be delayed a few more days before going home, and reminding her of her promise not to worry Ashley's family.

After shutting off her computer, she stowed it back in her laptop bag and looked around the table. It shocked her to realize that Max and Randy had left and she hadn't even noticed. Chris had slid over into the chair Max had occupied earlier, the one next to Dillon. They were both speaking in low tones to each other as Dillon wrote notes on a legal pad.

Chris glanced at his watch and shoved his chair back. "I guess I'll see you bright and early tomorrow at the office. Or are you working from here?"

"That depends on Ashley," Dillon said.

"I don't mind going to the office with you, if that's what you're asking."

Both men looked at her in surprise.

Dillon smiled and stood. "I thought you were still buried in that laptop of yours. Did you finish your report?"

"Yes. Finally. What about you two? Any progress?"

"Some. I'll catch you up in a few minutes. I'm going to lock the door behind Chris."

"Actually, can you give me a minute alone with Miss Parrish?" Chris asked.

Dillon's brows rose but he nodded and headed to the door. "I'll meet you on the porch."

"Thanks." Chris waited until the sounds of Dillon's boots on the hardwood floor faded before turning back toward Ashley. He crossed to her chair and took the seat beside her.

When he didn't immediately say anything, she teased him, "Let me guess. You want some tax advice, right? Happens all the time. People hear I'm a CPA and they think I can save them some money on their taxes."

His look turned thoughtful.

"That was a joke," she said.

"Yeah, I know. But still. Maybe you can save me some money. We'll have to talk about that later."

She shrugged. "Sure, I don't mind. What did you want to talk to me about now?"

A light flush colored his cheeks and he stared down

at his hands. "I, ah, wanted to thank you, actually." His dark eyes shot up to hers. "You saved my life this morning, on the boat. You saw that guy, the one you call Iceman, before anyone else did. If you hadn't tackled me, I'd be dead. The bullet went right through the boat's windshield, right where I was standing. Thank you is hardly adequate but, well, thank you."

"Are you kidding? I'm the one who owes you and the entire SWAT team my thanks. If you hadn't risked your lives and gone into Gibson and Gibson yesterday, I'd be dead right now, or at the very least, a prisoner of Iceman. And I'm not kidding myself that he wants to keep me alive long-term, so either way you did save my life. Thank you."

He seemed to sit a little straighter in his chair. "Well, I guess we're equal, then. We saved each other. But I still owe you a debt of gratitude. If you ever need anything, I'm there. All right? Just say the word. I mean it."

She put her hand on his where it rested on the table. "The one thing I could use right now is a friend."

He grinned. "Now, that I can do. See you tomorrow, friend."

Ashley called out to him when he reached the door. "Hey, Chris?"

He turned. "Yeah?"

"Do you like chocolate?"

A look of confusion crossed his face. "Who doesn't? Why?"

"Just wondering. Good night. See you tomorrow."

He nodded and headed out the door.

Ashley yawned. The past twenty-four hours were catching up to her. Even with the long nap she'd had, she was suddenly exhausted.

"Let me guess. You're too sleepy to stay up for dinner and to hear an update on the case, right?" Dillon stood in the opening of the room Ashley thought of as the library, his tone teasing.

"Actually, yes. I'm bushed, and not at all hungry. Maybe you can catch me up on the case tomorrow at the office?"

"No problem."

She put her laptop bag over her neck and shoulder again and stood, wincing at the pressure on her sore feet. Suddenly she was in Dillon's arms and he was carrying her back through the house.

"I really can walk now, you know. You don't have to keep carrying everywhere."

"It gives me an excuse to hold you," he teased. "I really don't mind."

"I don't mind, either," she breathed.

He shot her a surprised look, then frowned and carried her into the master bedroom, depositing her gently on the bed.

What had that frown meant?

"I'd like to leave around seven, if that's not too early," he said.

"Not at all. I'm an early riser. I'll be ready."

He glanced at the windows and frowned again. He made a circuit around the room, checking the locks on the windows and closing the heavy curtains.

"Dillon, the name of your farm, was that handed down through the generations, too?"

He slowly shook his head no.

"Well, it's a pretty name, Harmony Haven. How did you come up with that name?"

He stood like a stone, his mouth drawing into a tight line. The silence stretched out between them, turning awkward, the air charged with some indefinable emotion. Pain? Regret? Anger? Then, without answering, he left and closed the door behind him with a firm click.

Chapter Eight

The sun was barely up the next morning by the time Dillon finished his rounds of the barns and checked in with Griffin, who assured Dillon that he and his men understood the danger and would be on their guard in case Iceman somehow ended up here.

Satisfied he'd done everything he could to keep his home and workers safe, Dillon left his filthy boots in the mudroom at the back of the house, washed up in the utility sink and headed into the kitchen. He froze at the smell of warm chocolate and stared right into the smiling eyes of Ashley Parrish.

His kitchen, in the two hours since he'd left the house, had been transformed into a bakery. And the person responsible was standing right in the middle of the chaos in a pair of jeans, fluffy pink bunny slippers and an adorable "Kiss the Cook" apron, watching him warily, as if she expected him to yell at her.

He sighed and locked the door behind him. He owed her an apology for last night, but Harmony was one subject he had no intention of discussing with her. Ever. She was here on a temporary basis. She'd made that abundantly clear. And he wasn't going to share the memory of Harmony with someone who'd be gone in a few days.

The unexpected sadness that shot through him at that reminder—that this beautiful, spunky, smart woman would be out of his life so soon—bothered him far more than he cared to admit.

She set the mixing bowl she'd been holding back on the counter and bit her bottom lip. "I'm sorry if you're upset that I made a mess of your kitchen, and used your supplies from the pantry. But I'd hoped you wouldn't mind. I love to bake, and I thought I'd make something special to thank everyone at the police department for everything they've done, and are still doing for me. I couldn't find you this morning and thought you wouldn't..." Her shoulders slumped. "You're angry. I should have waited and asked permission."

He reached her in three long strides and put his hand beneath her chin, gently forcing her to look at him. "I'm not angry."

Her whiskey-colored eyes searched his. "You're not?"

"Not even a little bit. I'm just...surprised." He glanced at the mounds of muffins and cupcakes and cookies piled on plates in the middle of the table. "Are we hosting a party for five-year-olds and I forgot?"

She lightly shoved him. "Don't be silly. Adults love cookies and cupcakes, too. And it's not all junk food." She hurried over to a plate of dark bread and held it up. "I made some bran bread. It's healthy and tastes good, if you want to try it."

He joined her at the table but passed up the bran bread in favor of one of the chocolate chip cookies. He took a bite and closed his eyes as the warm, gooey chocolate-and-cookie mixture did a dance across his taste buds.

"Do you like it?" She sounded worried.

He opened his eyes. "Best cookie ever. I mean it. The guys at the office are going to go crazy over this."

She grinned and clapped her hands together. "Thank goodness. For a moment there, I thought I'd lost my touch."

The sheer delight on her face because her hard work would make others happy tilted his world for a moment, long enough for him to consider doing something he knew he'd regret. But he couldn't help himself.

He leaned down and kissed her. Her soft lips tasted like chocolate and honey, a heady combination that had him lingering when he knew he should stop—especially since she'd frozen like a surprised rabbit as soon as his lips touched hers.

Frustration curled inside him, but he broke the kiss and pulled back.

She threw her arms around his neck. "Don't you dare stop now."

His shock at her boldness turned to laughter as she tugged at his hair to make him lean down. He put his arms around her waist and lifted her up until she was at eye level.

"Demanding little thing, aren't you?" he whispered before his mouth met hers. He turned with her in his arms, intending to brace her against the tabletop, but she surprised him again by lifting her legs and wrapping them around his hips.

White-hot heat whipped through him and he groaned low in his throat. Her soft lips opened beneath his in an invitation he couldn't have resisted if the entire town was under siege and he was their only hope to save them.

Neither of them seemed inclined to stop. The kiss grew wild and his pants grew uncomfortably tight. When he realized he was seriously considering shoving all her cookies and cakes off the table so he could make love to her right then and there, he finally pulled the strength together to break the kiss.

Ashley clung to him, her eyelids half-closed, panting through her swollen lips, every breath pushing her soft, full breasts against his chest, making him want her even more.

"We have to stop," he whispered, even as he leaned down to kiss the tip of her perky little nose. He moved to her cheek next and licked the small spot of chocolate smeared on her soft skin.

She whimpered in the back of her throat and closed her eyes, leaning back against his arm and turning her head for his wandering mouth. Her sheer joy in life and her trust in him to hold her and keep her safe stunned him. What would she do if he took her to the bedroom right now? Would she welcome him? Or would she come to her senses and stop him?

He took a step toward the kitchen archway. Then another.

No, stop it. What was he doing? He might not know Ashley Parrish very well, but he didn't believe she was a one-night-stand kind of woman. And that meant Ashley Parrish was off-limits.

It almost killed him to pull back and set her away from him.

She looked up at him questioningly, her eyes so full of trust, that it hurt to meet her gaze. Once again, he owed her an explanation. But once again, that was more than he could bear.

"I'll grab a couple of boxes to help us carry all those cakes and cookies into the office." With that incredibly thin excuse, he hurried out of the kitchen and tried to convince himself he hadn't seen the hurt in her eyes when he turned away.

DILLON WASN'T SURE exactly how he'd expected Ashley to act once he'd showered and changed for work. But surely after that earth-tilting kiss they'd shared she should have looked at him differently, or even been angry because he'd ended the kiss so abruptly without a decent explanation. He sure hadn't expected her to act as if nothing had even happened. But that's what she'd done, happily chattering all the way to the office.

Apparently baking made her a chatty Cathy. Maybe she should have been a baker instead of an accountant, because talking about recipes made her animated like nothing else. She looked so adorable waving her hands around, her eyes sparkling as she discussed the right temperature to bake the perfect banana-nut bread. And damn if he didn't want to kiss her all over again.

Well, he'd managed not to make a fool of himself by kissing her again, but three hours after arriving at the office, he wasn't so sure bringing her here had been any better of an idea. From the moment he'd set the boxes of baked goods in the kitchenette, everyone had shoved him out of the way to get at the cookies, cakes and breads. And once they'd tasted the heaven of Ashley's homemade concoctions, she'd become an instant celebrity.

They'd passed her from desk to desk, asking her secrets and talking recipes until he'd had to order some of the worst offenders to leave her alone and get back to work. The chief had come out of his office to see what the noise was about, and after a brief conversation with Ashley, he'd led her into his office. That was more than forty-five minutes ago and they were still in there. What was the chief talking to her about? How to bake the perfect brownie?

Chris rolled his chair over to Dillon's desk. "You look angry enough to kill someone. What's up?"

"Nothing." He forced his gaze away from the chief's closed door and tried to focus on the interview report in front of him, one of the many interviews from survivors of the Gibson and Gibson shooting. He'd already read the interviews several times, but he was rereading them to see if he could pick up on anything he'd missed.

"Nothing, huh?" Chris teased. "I don't suppose nothing has something to do with one very perky little brunette living at your house right now?"

"Did you complete that background report on Todd Dunlop I asked you to do?"

Chris chuckled and rolled his chair back to his desk. A moment later he wheeled back over and plopped a thick manila file folder on top of the interview Dillon had been reading. "I was going to review it again before I gave it to you, but hey, since you're so anxious for it, here you go."

Dillon flipped the folder open. "Give me the highlights."

Chris propped his feet on the edge of the desk and leaned back with his hands folded behind his head. "Todd Dunlop, fifty-five years of age. Married, father of three adult children—two sons and a daughter. Entrepreneur, started Dunlop Enterprises fresh out of college, which was basically a logistics company that provided transportation and storage for smaller businesses that couldn't afford to rent a warehouse. In less than five years the company was bringing in over fifty million a year in revenue. Dunlop expanded and diversified and five years after that he became America's newest billionaire. Then, for reasons unknown, two days ago he went freaking nuts and walked into Gibson and Gibson shooting anything that moved. Killed eight, injured three more. And as we both know, he followed Ashley Parrish around the office like a hunter after a trophy buck."

Dillon thumbed through the remaining pages in the folder. "Why does a man with everything throw it all away and go on a murderous rampage? The coroner's tox screen came back clean. He wasn't drunk or high. So what gives? There has to be more to it than what you've got in this report." He tossed the stack of pages back on his desk. "We have to dig deeper. What about the widow and his children? Are they back from their trip to Europe yet?"

"I've left five messages with the wife's attorney. He's supposed to call as soon as they get back, and he hasn't called."

"Doesn't sound like a close, loving family if they don't want to cut their vacation short to find out why their loved one went on a shooting spree. For that matter, you'd think they would have at least inquired about taking the body for burial."

Chris shrugged. "Rich people are different than other people."

"No, they're not. They may hide behind their wealth and possessions, but at their core they're like everyone else. They love and hate like the rest of us. Someone in that family had to know something about the father. There are always signs before someone snaps. We need to push the family harder, get them in here for an interview."

The door to the chief's office opened. The chief stepped out with Ashley. He kissed her on the cheek and wiped his eyes.

"What the… Is the chief…crying?" Dillon asked.

Chris shook his head. "I never thought I'd see the day. What's going on?"

"I have no idea."

The chief held Ashley's hand and spoke to her in low tones. Ashley nodded and smiled. Dillon didn't have a clue what they were talking about, but he was determined to find out. He shoved his chair back just as the front door opened.

A man wearing a dark suit that screamed federal agent stepped inside and held the door open for a woman in a shiny orange suit that screamed money. Her faded red hair was streaked with gray, and diamonds dripped from her ears, throat and fingers.

"You are not going to believe who the woman in the peach silk suit is," Chris said.

"Who is she?"

Chris grabbed the folder he'd pitched on Dillon's desk and flipped through to the back. He pulled out a picture and slapped it on top. "This is a picture of Todd Dunlop's wife. Look familiar?"

The picture was taken years ago but there was no mistaking the similarities. "Patricia Dunlop. The widow has finally arrived. What's she doing with a federal agent?"

"What makes you think he's a fed?" Chris asked.

"Cheap suit, white shirt, black tie. And he's way too pretty to make it as a regular cop. We'd eat him for breakfast."

"I think you're wrong. I think he's her lawyer," Chris said.

"Fifty bucks?"

"You're on."

Dillon and Chris started across the room. At the same time, the woman turned and pointed at Ashley.

"There she is," she said, in a voice dripping with

venom. She marched over to Ashley, leaving the suit to chase after her. She stopped directly in front of her. "That's the woman who ruined our company and killed my husband." She drew back her fist and punched Ashley across the face.

ASHLEY HELD THE ice pack to her throbbing cheek and warily eyed the woman who was arguing with the chief on the other side of the room.

"Are you sure you're okay?" Dillon asked, crouching in front of her chair.

"Okay is relative, I suppose. At least she didn't knock out any teeth."

Dillon's mouth tightened into a thin line. "Let me arrest her for assault. She deserves to be locked up for what she did to you."

She lowered the ice pack and placed it on top of the desk. "No. She doesn't. She just lost her husband. No matter what he did, it's as much a shock to her as everyone else. Her whole world has been destroyed."

"She's a billionaire. I hardly think her world has been destroyed, but I get the point." He sighed heavily. "All right. I won't arrest her. For now. But if you change your mind, let me know."

"I won't."

He smiled. "Yeah. I figured. By the way, before Cruella de Vil showed up, what were you doing in the chief's office so long?"

"Taxes."

"Taxes?"

She nodded and picked the ice pack up. "I told him about some deductions he's been missing. If he amends his past returns, he'll probably get about ten thousand dollars back." She held the ice against her cheek, hoping to numb the pain.

Dillon grinned. "I should have known it was about money. That's the only thing that would make the chief cry." He pressed a kiss against her forehead and stood. "I'll see if I can get to the bottom of this mess. Chris will watch over you until I get back."

Ashley blinked in surprise at the unexpected kiss as Dillon walked away and joined the chief on the other side of the room. She tore her gaze away from Dillon when Chris rolled his chair up beside her.

"Don't worry. We've all got your back. Cops are like stray cats—feed them once and they'll love you forever." He leaned in close, his expression turning serious for once. "But watch out for Dillon. He's more of a brother to me than my own brothers could ever be, which means I know him better than anyone else, except maybe his mother."

She lowered the ice pack again. "I don't understand. What do you mean, watch out for him?"

"He's a sucker for hard-luck cases, which makes you darn near irresistible. But don't expect him to ever be able to commit to anything. He suffered a terrible loss and blames himself. He's a wreck inside. I'm just saying, I saw the way he was looking at you earlier. And I can count on one hand the number of women he's ever kissed, no matter how innocent, in front of anyone else. If you encourage him, you'll only end up hurt. And so will he."

She was about to protest that she had no intention of pursuing a relationship with Dillon when a commotion had both of them looking toward the front of the room. Patricia Dunlop aimed a glare Ashley's way, then stalked out the front door. The man who'd come in with her looked noticeably relieved when she left.

Dillon left the small group huddled around the stranger and came back to Ashley. Tiny lines at the corners of his eyes broadcast the tension in him when he stopped in front of her.

"Ashley, you need to come to the chief's office."

She put the ice pack down again. "Okay, but why? What's going on?"

"Yeah, spill, buddy," Chris said from his seat beside her.

"That man in the suit, the one who came in with Mrs. Dunlop, is Special Agent Jason Kent. He's with the FBI and he's investigating a string of embezzlement cases. He's here to arrest you."

Chapter Nine

Ashley shook her head and looked around the room. She was sitting in Chief Thornton's office with the chief, Chris, Dillon and the FBI agent. But it felt more as though she was in the middle of a horrible nightmare that wouldn't end.

"I don't understand," she said. "You're accusing me of stealing millions of dollars from companies I never even worked for."

Special Agent Kent held up the briefcase he'd brought with him. "I have extensive reports in here that say you did. Your name is all over the audits that were performed on these companies."

"But that's not possible. Could there be another Ashley Parrish out there? That has to be it. You have me confused with someone else."

He rattled off a Social Security number. "That's the number the auditor gave to each company when they made checks out to her for services rendered. Sound familiar?"

She fisted her hands in her lap. "Well, yes, it's mine, but that doesn't mean anything. Someone must have stolen my identity."

"And performed audits, under your name, for over

a year? People generally steal identities to pilfer credit cards and get into people's bank accounts. Your typical identity thief wouldn't be able to fake an audit, and honestly, that sounds ridiculously farfetched."

Dillon leaned forward in his chair. "Maybe, maybe not. You did say the auditor was able to embezzle millions of dollars. That's a heck of a carrot for someone with auditing skills to put in the work to steal Miss Parrish's identity."

Kent's sharp gaze zeroed in on Dillon like a laser-guided missile. "Are we speaking about the same Miss Parrish that you kissed a few minutes ago? I hardly think you're an unbiased party in this matter."

Dillon's jaw went rigid. "A peck on the forehead is hardly a kiss. And I don't exactly think you can claim you're unbiased, since you walked in here with one of the alleged victims in the embezzlement case."

This time it was the FBI agent's turn to look angry. His brows drew down and he narrowed his eyes at Dillon. "Mrs. Dunlop is one of many witnesses I've questioned in the course of this investigation. When word of the shooting reached our office in Knoxville and I found out one of the survivors was listed as Ashley Parrish, I called Mrs. Dunlop. I asked if she'd accompany me down here so she could make a positive ID so I could arrest Miss Parrish. And of course, I offered condolences on her husband's death."

"Her husband the shooter, right? We're talking about the same man who killed eight people and tried to kill Miss Parrish?" Dillon gritted out.

"More to my point, Detective. Have you been able to find a motive behind the shooting?" He paused and watched Dillon. "From your expression, I'm guessing the answer is no. How does five million dollars, which also happened to destroy Dunlop's financial empire, sound as a motive? Mr. Dunlop might have been a billionaire on paper, but his company was going through tough economic times and was severely in debt. The five million dollars that disappeared from the company's accounts—after Miss Parrish's audit—wiped out the company's liquidity. They couldn't make payroll and had to file for bankruptcy last week. A couple of days before Mr. Dunlop's murderous rampage at Gibson and Gibson. It's no wonder his widow blames Miss Parrish for her husband's death."

The room went silent and all eyes seemed to focus on Ashley.

She threw her hands in the air in a helpless gesture. "But I never worked for Dunlop Enterprises. And I've never even seen Mrs. Dunlop before."

Kent reached into his suit jacket and pulled a picture from his pocket. "Is this your picture, Miss Parrish?"

She stared at the black-and-white photo of her in a business suit, smiling at the camera. "Yes," she whispered. "But I've never seen that picture before."

"Really?" He plopped it on the chief's desk. "I find that hard to believe, since it's on the home page of your company website."

She dragged her gaze from the photograph back to the agent. "What?"

"You did create an LLC under your name, correct?"

"Well, yes. I'm self-employed, so registering myself as a limited liability company makes sense. Of course I—"

"And you have a website?" He rattled off a URL.

She shook her head. "No, no. I don't have a website. I've never needed one. Most of my cases are referrals from other clients."

"I've got signed affidavits from six different companies you performed audits on in the past twelve months. Every one of them had hundreds of thousands of dollars stolen from their accounts right after you performed your audits. You're telling me that's a coincidence?"

She glanced around the room, but no one would look her in the eye anymore. She swallowed against the thick lump in her throat. "You have to believe me. I've never heard of any of the companies you mentioned at the start of this meeting. I don't have a website. I've never seen that picture before. I don't...I don't know what else to say, except that if you think an auditor has access to company accounts, you don't have a clue what an auditor does. I rarely even get a log-on ID when I audit a company. They provide me printouts, statements, company financial records, which I review. That's it. I couldn't embezzle from them even if I wanted to."

"I agree, which is why this case puzzled me for so long. I eventually came up with the theory that you must have found a weak link at the companies you embezzled from. An employee with access to the accounts, perhaps someone you blackmailed because you found evidence of mismanagement or wrongdoing. Rather than report it in your audit, you used the evidence against the employee to get them to give you company funds."

"I'm hearing a lot of conjecture," the chief said, rapping his fist on his desk. "But I've yet to see one iota of proof against Miss Parrish."

"My entire briefcase is loaded with proof, but I'll make this easy for all of you." He looked at each one of them until they were all focused on him. "You had another shooting, aside from the one at Gibson and Gibson. A shooting involving Miss Parrish, correct?"

The chief shot Dillon a surprised glance before looking back at Kent. "Yes, we did. We killed one of the shooters but haven't established an ID on him yet. The other one is still at large."

"Perhaps I can help you with that." Kent pulled another picture out of his pocket and held it up for them to see before placing it on the desk.

Ashley drew in a sharp breath as recognition slammed into her. "Baldy," she whispered.

"What's his name?" Dillon demanded.

"Keith Johnson. He worked for one of the companies Miss Parrish audited. He had direct access to the company's accounts. I'm guessing she cut him out of the profits and he went looking for revenge, or perhaps he wanted to force her to give him his share. Makes sense, since he didn't try to kill her. He only tried to abduct her."

The chief glanced at Ashley, then looked away.

"I swear, I never saw that man before that night on Cooper's Bluff," Ashley said, watching Dillon, hoping he would look at her.

But he didn't. Instead, he stared at the picture on the desk.

Kent held up another picture.

Ashley clasped her hand to her throat as she stared into the cold, dead eyes of Iceman.

"This man is Luther Kennedy. I'm willing to bet he's your second shooter." He looked at Dillon, who gave him a crisp nod.

"Luther is more or less a thug, with a history of charges that never stuck. But for some reason, Todd Dunlop trusted him. He was his right-hand man. He handled security and a host of other tasks for Mr. Dunlop, with full access to his accounts. He's one of only a handful of people who could have funneled money out of the accounts of Dunlop Enterprises. We believe he must have been Mr. Dunlop's go-between, personally carrying company papers to the woman who was auditing the company. Ashley Parrish."

"Obviously Luther's the hired hand," Dillon said, "but what makes you so sure he's the one who accessed the accounts and worked with…the auditor on the side? You mentioned a handful of people could have funneled the money out."

"Yes, but only one of them had motive. The handful of people includes Dunlop's wife, daughter and two sons, all of whom live a wealthy, pampered lifestyle with no motive to try to steal Todd Dunlop's money. But Luther, even though Dunlop relied heavily on him, was given only a moderate salary. He had financial problems and bad credit, and toward the end, before Todd Dunlop went on his rampage, witnesses said Luther and Todd argued a lot. One witness even said Luther asked Todd for a loan and was refused. After ten years of being his errand boy, that had to sting. Let's face it. The only one with access *and* motive is Luther Kennedy."

Special Agent Kent plopped the picture of Iceman down on the growing stack of pictures on the chief's desk. "Look, Destiny is a small town, with a few thousand residents. I understand you don't get complicated cases very often, not like we do in Knoxville. And it's perfectly understandable you wouldn't connect the dots like I did. You don't have the resources out here in the country, or the experience, but I do. And I've already done the legwork. I'm not here to convince you. I'm here to take Miss Parrish into custody."

This time all eyes focused on Agent Kent, and their gazes weren't friendly.

He cleared his throat, his face turning slightly red.

"That didn't come out the way I meant it to. I wasn't trying to criticize your abilities."

The chief straightened in his chair and smiled. "Of course not. Think nothing of it. This office has always had an exemplary relationship with the feds and I'm sure you wouldn't intentionally do anything to jeopardize our long-standing tradition of cooperation. How about we start all over? No one offered you coffee when you came in, did they? How do you like it? Black?"

Kent relaxed against his chair, looking relieved. "Actually, some cream and sugar would be great. Thank you, Chief Thornton. I appreciate your understanding in this matter."

"Of course, of course. It's not like we'd try to give you the runaround, or turn a blind eye. Chris, go get Agent Kent that coffee. Make it quick."

Chris almost knocked his chair down in his eagerness to leave the office. He hurried out and shut the door behind him.

"Agent Kent, why don't you set that briefcase up here on my desk? If you've got information that can help me clear the Gibson and Gibson shooting as well as the Cooper's Bluff fiasco out of my in-box, I'm all for it. Show me what you've got."

Kent glanced at Ashley. "I don't think the suspect should be privy to all of this information."

"Right, what was I thinking? You know us country folk. Not used to how you do things in the big city."

Ashley detected an edge to his voice and wondered if Kent had picked up on it, too.

"Detective Gray," the chief said, "get Miss Parrish out of here, please. And if I don't see you before you leave on vacation, give your mama my best."

Dillon shot to his feet and grabbed Ashley's arm, pulling her to her feet, as well. "Will do, Chief. Nice to meet you, Special Agent Kent."

"Nice to meet you, too."

Ashley's mouth fell open. She couldn't believe this was happening. She looked up at Dillon, but he was stone-faced and silent as he pulled her toward the door.

The door opened and Chris stood there with a cup of coffee in his hand. He gave a slight nod to Dillon before hurrying inside without looking at Ashley.

Dillon pulled the door shut behind them and leaned down next to her ear. "Hurry, we probably only have a few minutes."

"What? What do you mean?" She stumbled trying to keep up with his long strides. Her feet, though much better, were still sore.

He immediately slowed and let go of her forearm. His fingers instead entwined with hers as he pulled her toward the door.

Ashley glanced around in confusion. Everyone in the squad room had their backs to her, as if they were purposely avoiding looking her way. Her cheeks grew hot and her stomach clenched into a hard, cold knot.

"What happened while I was in the chief's office? Did Chris tell everyone I'm a thief? Now they all hate me."

Dillon stopped at the door and looked back at his fellow officers. For the first time since the nightmare in the chief's office had begun, he smiled. "No, they don't hate you. They're showing you their solidarity. They're turning a blind eye."

She frowned. "A blind eye?"

His grin widened. "Yep. And now I've got to start my formerly unplanned vacation."

"I don't understand. What are you talking about?"

"We're about to give Special Agent Kent the runaround."

Chapter Ten

Ashley sat on Dillon's bed while he shoved the folders he'd grabbed from his library into a duffel bag that was much like hers, except that his was camouflage-green.

"Are you absolutely sure Chief Thornton is okay with this?" Ashley asked. "I wouldn't want you to lose your job or anything."

He paused in front of her. "Do you remember the chief saying he had a long tradition of cooperating with the feds? Well, trust me, he's *never* cooperated with the feds. He's old-school, resents their interference. Me, I never had a problem with them, until now." He turned and opened another drawer in his dresser.

"So he was speaking some kind of code then? When he talked about turning a blind eye and giving someone the runaround and you going on vacation, he was telling you to take off with me and hide me?"

"Pretty much."

"But isn't that illegal?"

"It violates the spirit of the law but not the letter. Agent Kent never got around to arresting you. And he didn't serve you or anyone else with a subpoena or a warrant. So technically, all we did was have a conversation. I'm now on vacation, and I happened to take you with me. You're a witness in an investigation whose life is in danger until we catch Luther Kennedy. So the chief can argue later that you're just in protective custody."

"Sounds dicey to me. I'd red flag that like crazy in an audit."

He laughed. "Yeah, I probably would, too."

He shoved a thin blanket into the duffel bag and zipped it closed.

"Dillon? Why are you helping me? All those things that man said about me… If it wasn't happening to me, if he'd said that about someone else, I'd believe him. Why are you helping me, and why is the chief helping me?"

He plopped down on the bed beside her, making the mattress bounce.

"Honestly, the chief is probably responding more to Kent's denigration of us country folk than to anything else. He doesn't appreciate city slickers coming in here and acting like we're a bunch of idiots because we talk slow and there's only one red light in town. He's protecting his investigation more than anything else. He'll be pushing Chris and the others to figure out exactly what's going on, hoping to show up the FBI and prove the local yokels can out-investigate the feds."

"I guess that makes a little more sense than blind faith in me, since we basically just met. What about you? Are you helping me because you want to prove Destiny cops are as good investigators as federal ones? I'd appreciate your honesty."

"My honesty?" His gaze slid away from hers and he stared toward the front window, but Ashley didn't think he was seeing anything outside. His gaze was turned more inward, as if he was remembering something. Or someone.

"Honestly, I don't know what's going on, what you're

in the middle of," he finally said, his voice low, halting. "My instincts tell me to trust you, that you're innocent. But the evidence says otherwise. The only thing I'm sure of right now is that you need protection. I'm not going to turn you over to anyone until I'm sure you'll be safe. We're going to get out of here and lie low until everything is sorted out. Once Luther is in custody and the investigation is over, if the evidence shows you're guilty, I'll put you in a cell myself." His gaze slid back to hers. "How's that for honesty?"

She swallowed against the lump in her throat. "I guess I asked for that, didn't I?"

He put his hand beneath her chin and tilted her head up.

"If you're innocent, you've got nothing to fear, not from me or the law, anyway. Okay?"

She pushed his hand away. "Okay."

He frowned and looked as though he was going to add something else, but the squawk of a radio filled the room.

"John Wayne and Daisy Duke, this is Billy the Kid. Come in. Over."

He rolled his eyes and grabbed a small black phone-looking device with an antenna off the top of his dresser. It reminded Ashley of the walkie-talkies she and her siblings played with as children, but the device Dillon was holding looked a lot more sophisticated.

"This is John Wayne," Dillon said. "Over."

"Rosco P. Coltrane is ticked off like you wouldn't believe. And he's smarter than he looks. Boss Hogg advises you to get out of Dodge ASAP."

"Ten four, *Billy Bob.*"

"Ah, negative. This is Billy the Kid. No Billy Bob

here. Estimate you have fifteen minutes, tops, to make your getaway."

Dillon cursed. "Got it. Thanks. Over."

He shoved the walkie-talkie into the side zipper pouch on his duffel bag.

"Was that Chris?" Ashley asked.

"Yep."

"And you understood that?"

"Yep. He said Special Agent Kent figured out I was hiding you and he's ticked about it. He's on his way. He'll be here in fifteen minutes. Chief Thornton told us to get out of here before Kent gets here." He tossed the duffel over his shoulder and grabbed her duffel off the foot of the bed.

"So I'm Daisy Duke?"

He cocked a brow. "Only if you want to be."

She grinned. "Abso-freakin-lutely."

"HORSES? WE'RE MAKING our getaway on horses?" She was wearing a pair of borrowed boots, while Dillon and his farm manager, Griffin, saddled Dillon's stallion and a mare. Apparently with the expectation that she and Dillon were actually going to ride the darn things.

Dillon pressed his knee into the mare's side, forcing her to blow out a breath so he could cinch the saddle more tightly. "You have a better idea?"

"Well, yeah. When you moved your car out behind the shed, I figured we were going to head down some private road at the back of your property that no one else knows about."

"Nope, there's no secret road out here. And everyone in Blount County knows my bright red Jeep. We can't risk Kent seeing it since it was parked in front of the police station when he got there. Too obvious."

"And riding a horse isn't?"

"Not where we're going." He narrowed his eyes at her. "You *have* ridden a horse before, haven't you?"

"Sure. When I was fifteen."

"It's like riding a bike, ma'am," Griffin called out. "You'll remember how."

Dillon nodded, as if Griffin had quoted some sage advice. "Plus, Gracie here is an old trail mare. As long as she has a horse in front of her to follow, she won't give you any trouble."

He finished securing Ashley's duffel bag behind the saddle and turned around. "Need a leg up?" He bent down and cupped his hands. "Or are your feet too sore? I could lift you up."

Ashley stiffened. "I can mount all by myself, thank you very much." She put her boot in the stirrup, grabbed the saddle horn and hoisted herself up. She swung her right leg over the mare's back and gently settled into the saddle, all in one quick, smooth motion.

Dillon's brows rose. "I thought you said you hadn't ridden since you were fifteen."

"I haven't. But I might have neglected to mention that I was in a saddle since before I could walk and have so many riding trophies on my mom's mantel the fake-gold paint practically blinds you when you walk into the house."

She expected him to laugh, or accuse her of being a ringer. But instead his expression turned serious.

"Your mom's mantel, huh? Imagine that." He strode to the bay-colored stallion Griffin had finished saddling, the one Dillon had told her he'd named Boomerang. He gracefully and expertly mounted the horse, making Ashley feel like an amateur.

"Nice form," she grudgingly complimented.

He gave her a curt nod.

The two-way radio crackled again. “Billy the Kid calling John Wayne. Over.”

Griffin’s old, wrinkled face split into a wide grin. “Is that Chris?”

“I’m humoring him,” Dillon muttered. He held up the walkie. “Go ahead, Billy. Over.”

“Annie Oakley spotted Rosco P. Coltrane headed your way, two minutes out.”

A pained look crossed Dillon’s face. “Is Annie Oakley someone I know?”

“You see her every day, Mr. Wayne.”

“Got it. Tell Annie thanks for the warning. Over.” Dillon shoved the radio into a holder he’d strung around the saddle horn in front of him.

“Who’s Annie?” Ashley asked.

“I’m guessing Officer Donna Waters. She’s the only woman I see every day. Griffin?”

“Yeah, I know, Boss. I never saw either of you.”

“That would make it hard to explain my Jeep if anyone looks around. Just tell the truth, that you don’t know where we’re going. Because you don’t.”

Griffin nodded and ran to the sliding doors at the back of the barn facing away from the house. He slid one of the tall, heavy doors open, revealing a breathtaking view of the mountains. But separating the barn from those mountains was a deep green, open field.

“Come on,” Dillon urged. “Let’s go.”

Ashley nudged her mount over beside Dillon’s. “But there’s no cover. Agent Kent will see us if we go that way.”

“That’s why we’re not going that way.” He pointed out the door to the right. Acres and acres of tall cornstalks waved in the afternoon breeze. His mouth quirked up in a grin. “Let’s see if you earned those riding trophies honestly or not. Try to keep up.”

He kicked his heels into Boomerang’s side and the stallion took off in a gallop. Before Ashley could do more than blink, he disappeared into the cornfield.

“Keep up. Keep up? I’ll show you keep up.” She kicked her mount and took off in pursuit.

LUTHER ADJUSTED HIS position on the rocky outcrop in the mountains high above Harmony Haven and trained his binoculars on the FBI agent far below. Special Agent Jason Kent had been a burr in Luther’s side for months now. It was kind of nice seeing the agent have so much difficulty for a change.

Kent raised his hands in the air, obviously angry and frustrated as he talked to another man in front of the barn behind the house where Detective Gray and Ashley Parrish had been a few minutes ago. He whirled around and marched to his car parked on the side of the house. A cloud of dust spit up from his wheels as he punched the accelerator and drove back the way he’d come. The FBI agent was too dumb to take a harder look around. If he had, he would have discovered Gray’s red Jeep parked behind one of the outbuildings, not visible from the road. Kent hadn’t even considered that Gray and Parrish might have gotten away on horseback.

But Luther had no such affliction.

He’d seen them race out of the back of the barn and hightail it into the cornfield. And from his vantage point, he could see all four corners of that same field. All he had to do now was wait.

Sure enough, a few minutes later at the northeast corner, two horses and riders emerged from the waving dried-up stalks, moving at a fast clip toward a cluster of pine trees. Luther fondled the rifle in his hand. Tough shot from here, lots of variables—long distance, wind, heat, the unpredictability of horses who might shy or move sideways at any time. If he missed, he'd alert his prey he was following them. And while killing Gray wouldn't bother him one bit, Gray was riding too close to Parrish to take the shot. He decided the risk wasn't worth it. He needed Parrish alive.

At least for a little while.

He rubbed his aching shoulder. He wasn't sure old Doc Brookes had done his best work with a gun held to his head. But at least he could use his arm again and the doc had given him pain pills to dull the ache. The bullet had only grazed him, so all he'd needed was stitches and disinfectant. Still, it had hurt like the devil. Parrish would pay for that. Once his friend's scheme was done, Parrish would be all his. He'd carve out his pound of flesh.

And *then* he'd kill her.

Chapter Eleven

Dillon locked the cabin door and dropped the duffel bags onto the wood floor at the end of the couch, which—aside from a coffee table—was the only piece of furniture in the small space.

Ashley turned in a slow circle, her lack of enthusiasm evident in the tightening of her mouth, the slump of her shoulders. "Is this your cabin?"

"No. It belongs to a friend. He rarely uses it and told me where the spare key is in case I ever want to use it, which I do, during hunting season."

"Are we staying here tonight?"

"That depends on Rosco P. Coltrane and whether he figures out we're here." He set the radio on the bar that separated the tiny kitchen from the main room of the cabin. "The couch does fold out into a fairly comfortable bed if we stay. And there's a bathroom with a shower behind that door over there. But that's pretty much it."

She plopped down on the couch. "What do we do now?"

"I'll unsaddle the horses and set them up on lunge lines so they can graze. After that, I figure we can put our heads together and discuss the case. I'm going to call Chris and see if he can give me more details on what Kent thinks he has against you. Sound good?"

"I suppose. Do you need help with the horses?"

"I've got it. It'll only take me a few minutes. Lock the door behind me."

ASHLEY PULLED HER feet up and sat cross-legged on the couch, staring down at the mass of paper and folders Dillon had spread out before them on the coffee table. He sat beside her, making lists, grilling her with questions.

He glanced at her legs. "You okay? Do your feet hurt? I can put more salve and fresh bandages on them."

"They don't hurt. Just shifting position."

He cocked his head and studied one of the two-columned lists he'd just finished. "From what you've told me, we should be able to prove you were in completely different states at the time three of these audits Kent told us about were performed. I'll get Chris to check out the hotel records and dates."

"That's a good thing, right? Doesn't that give me an alibi?"

He tapped his pen. "Maybe. Can you audit someone long-distance, without physically going to their company?"

"Yes, in theory. It's frowned upon, not recommended. And I've certainly never done it."

"But it can be done."

Her shoulders slumped. "Yes. It can."

"Then we still have no proof that you weren't involved in this scam." He picked up the list of companies he'd written down during his talk with Chris on the phone earlier. "It's interesting that whoever pretended to be you performed audits on a lot of companies they didn't embezzle from."

"Why is that interesting? It just shows the audits didn't yield discrepancies the fake Ashley Parrish could use to blackmail someone, right? That is, if we buy what Special Agent Kent said about what was happening."

"True." He leafed through one of the folders and frowned. He pulled another one toward him and compared some pages from each.

Ashley leaned forward. "Did you find something else?"

"More like a new avenue of questions."

She plopped back against the couch cushions. "Great. More questions. Go ahead. Ask."

He turned to face her, resting one arm on the back of the couch. "I think we're going about this all wrong. We've been focusing on proving you're innocent instead of trying to figure out who's guilty. Let's assume you're innocent and move from there."

"Gee. Thanks."

He smiled. "If this is a scheme, which we're assuming, and someone stole your identity, they're passing themselves off as a real auditor. The only red flags being raised are that after the audits are complete, money goes missing. What kind of person could fake an audit that passes muster, that no one complains about?"

Ashley blinked as the obvious conclusion dawned on her. "They have to be a real auditor, a CPA, or at least have been educated as one."

"I agree." He grabbed a notebook and pen off the table and started a new list. The first bullet said "Auditor, or trained as one."

"Our bad guy also knows your Social Security number, and enough personal information to have faked a convincing-looking website under your name. Tell me about the picture Kent said came from that website. Are you sure you've never seen it before?"

"Pretty sure. I mean, I don't live near my family anymore. It's not like I get my picture taken very often."

"Where is your family?"

"Sweetwater."

"Tennessee, just outside Chattanooga?"

"That's it."

"Far enough to keep your family from dropping in unexpectedly, but not so far you can't go home if you need to?"

"Am I that easy to figure out?"

"No." His mouth quirked sardonically. "You're just a lot like me. I did the same thing. Left home the day I graduated high school, went away to college to put some distance between me and my family. I never intended to come back."

"But you did. You were going to be a vet, right? What happened?"

His smile faded. "Life happened. Let's get back to the case. I think it's logical to assume that whoever stole your identity knows you very well—well enough to be able to take a picture of you without you thinking anything about it, someone who would have access to your personal papers so they could find your Social Security number and other personal information, someone who was trained as an auditor." He added a bullet item to his list.

"I also suspect they must not have been very successful as an auditor in their own right, or they wouldn't have tried to use your reputation and identity to get clients. As we discussed earlier, a lot of the audits this person performed didn't raise any red flags with the FBI, and weren't precursors to embezzlement. That kind of strikes me as someone who was trying to make a living as an auditor but couldn't manage to get clients off their own reputation. So they used your reputation to get a foot in the door. The embezzling came later." He wrote another entry on his list.

"To get around using your identity, this person performed audits remotely. That strikes me as a way for them to get around the whole fake-website thing."

Ashley frowned. "I don't understand."

"If they used your name and their picture, they couldn't blame you later, or frame you, really, if things went bad. To cover themselves, they used your picture. But by doing that, they forced themselves to have to do the audits long-distance, so none of their clients actually saw them."

"But what about Mrs. Dunlop? She supposedly saw the auditor, and pointed at me and said I was the one who'd worked on the audit."

He shook his head. "I'm not sure I agree with that statement. All Mrs. Dunlop said was that you were the woman who'd killed her husband. She never once said she'd actually seen you in person. Maybe Kent jumped the gun on that and gave too much credence to a grieving widow who blamed you for her husband's death. It wouldn't be the first time a witness stretched the truth when they believed the person they were identifying was really guilty."

"Well, that's kind of a scary thought."

"That's one of many reasons cops don't rely solely on eyewitness testimony. Even without a motive to lie, a witness often truly believes in their testimony, even if their testimony is dead wrong. Eyewitness accounts are notoriously inaccurate. It's human nature not to remember a face well enough to later make a positive ID, especially after seeing other pictures of that person."

He passed her the list he'd made. "Is there anyone in your life, or anyone you've ever met in the past, maybe even someone you considered to be a friend, who meets all that criteria? Someone who knows what client accounts you take so they don't end up approaching the same clients? Someone who knows where you'll be at any given time? Someone you may trust?"

A sick feeling settled in the pit of Ashley's stomach. "Oh, my God."

Dillon narrowed his eyes. "You think you have a suspect?"

She nodded and handed the legal pad back to him. "There's only one person I can think of who knows me that well. She only studied accounting in college after I started studying it. She struggled all the way through, barely passing, no matter how much I tried to help her. And later, when my company took off, she was still struggling to get her first client." She pressed her hand to her throat. "She moved away a year and a half ago, saying she needed a new start. And suddenly she calls me to tell me *her* business is taking off. She's getting clients now and finally making a good living as an auditor. I was surprised, but happy for her. And she started going on trips and cruises, things she never could have afforded in the past."

Dillon reached for her hand. "Ashley, who is she?"

She swallowed hard, and squeezed her eyes shut. "My best friend since kindergarten, the same woman who called you the night I was abducted. Lauren Wilkes."

THE THEORY THAT her best friend had perpetrated such an awful fraud against Ashley was enough to make sleep nearly impossible for her. But surprisingly, it wasn't thoughts of Lauren's possible betrayal that were keeping her awake.

It was the fact that she was sharing a bed with Dillon.

Sleeping with him should have been awkward because they'd only known each other for a couple of days. And it *was* awkward, but for an entirely different reason. It was awkward because it *should* have felt wrong, but it felt totally…*right.* And if Ashley was certain he would welcome her interest in him, she'd be in his arms right now.

She wanted him, desperately. She wanted to reach out and slide her fingers over his skin, feel his muscles bunch beneath her touch. She wanted to explore the fascinating angles of his face, experience the raspy feel of his stubble gently abrading her skin as he explored her body. And more than anything right now, she wanted to feel him inside her, loving her, and for a little while at least, making her forget all her troubles.

Her skin grew heated and her fingers ached from clenching them together to keep from reaching for him. What was wrong with her? She'd never yearned for a man's touch like this. What was it about Dillon that made her feel so…out of control? Maybe a cold shower was what she needed. Anything would be better than this torture.

She flipped back the covers and started to get up.

Dillon's strong arm immediately wrapped around her waist, trapping her, pushing her back down. The bed dipped as he rose above her, leaned over her. The moonlight filtering through the thin curtains revealed far too much of his glorious body, naked from the waist up, and had her digging her nails into her palms to stop from reaching for him.

"What's wrong? Did you hear something outside?" He turned his face toward the window, as if to listen for whatever had disturbed her.

"No," she whispered. "I didn't hear anything. I… couldn't sleep." As if of their own will, her hands reached up and feathered across the stubble on his jaw.

He sucked in a breath, but didn't pull away.

Feeling as if she'd been granted a treasure, a magical moment to satisfy her curiosity, she continued her exploration. She slid her hungry fingers down the side of his neck, lower, over the hard contours of his chest, lower still, to the tautness of his stomach muscles, which jumped beneath her touch. She hesitated, her gaze locked with his, waiting, wondering what he would do if she moved her hands…lower.

"Don't stop now," he whispered, his voice ragged, deeper than usual.

Those three words were the key that unlocked a floodgate of pent-up frustration and emotion. Ashley didn't hesitate again. She slid her hands down to the waistband of the jeans he'd worn to bed, then groaned in frustration when she couldn't get past that barrier. She plucked at the top button, but her hands were shaking so hard she couldn't get it undone.

Dillon laughed and sat back, his thighs trapping hers as he made quick work of the button and zipper. He rolled to the side and lifted his hips to shuck off his pants and underwear. Ashley followed, her eager fingers searching for their prize.

He sucked in a sharp breath when she wrapped her hands around him.

"Ashley, wait, not so fast. We have plenty of—" He arched off the bed when her mouth covered him. His hands fisted in her hair and he shuddered beneath her.

She couldn't believe how perfect he was, how hot and hard. He must have been lying awake thinking of her like she'd been thinking of him.

She couldn't seem to get enough of him—his smell, his heat, his delicious salty taste. He shuddered again and she could feel he was close. Suddenly he bent down and wrapped his arms beneath hers and pulled her off him. She cursed in frustration and reached for him again.

He gave a pained laugh and pulled her hand away, then rolled and trapped her beneath him. He grabbed her wrists in a viselike grip and pulled them up above her head.

"If you don't stop," he said, his voice hoarse, "I'm going to disgrace myself like a randy teenager. Slow. Down."

"But I want—"

"So do I. But I want to last. I want to make this good for you, too."

He reached down and pulled her shirt off over her head, then expertly removed her jeans and panties until she was naked, too. Then he covered her with his body and captured her lips with his in an open-mouthed, ravenous kiss she felt all the way to her toes.

Every stroke of his tongue against hers sent a wave of heat straight to her belly. She was so ready for him she thought she might die if he didn't take her right then. She was about to demand he do so when he slid down, his stubble against her breasts her only warning before he sucked her nipple into his mouth.

She cried out and bucked beneath him, but he was unmerciful in his assault on her senses. He lavished both her breasts with careful attention until she was aching with the pleasure-pain of it. And then he leaned up until his hot breath washed over her neck.

"My turn," he breathed.

She shivered at his dark promise, and then he slid down her body and fastened his mouth on the very core of her. Her climax was immediate, an explosion of pleasure that flared across every nerve ending in her body, bowing her spine off the bed. He continued to explore and worship her with his mouth and tongue until she begged him to stop.

He kissed her there once, twice, before pulling away. The bed creaked and bounced as he leaned over and reached for something.

"What are you doing," she whispered. "Come back to me. I want—"

"Not half as much as I want, believe me. But I have to protect you."

She lifted her head and saw he'd grabbed his wallet. The moonlight glinted off the foil packet in his hand and she dropped her head back on the pillow. Thank goodness one of them had stopped to think about protection. She'd been far too gone to care.

Before her heart had even slowed from her climax he was back, his sweat-slicked skin sliding against hers as he trapped her mouth again for another earth-shattering, wet kiss. The length of him rubbed against her thigh and she whimpered against him. She sucked his tongue and he groaned.

He reached down between them and positioned himself at her entrance, and then he pushed himself into her, slowly, stretching her, filling her, until she whimpered against him and drew her knees up, desperate to pull him all the way inside.

He withdrew again, then pushed deeper, withdrew,

then deeper still, his every movement so exquisite, so delicious it was the sweetest form of torture.

"What are you doing to me, Dillon," she gasped.

"I think…it's…the other way…around," he rasped, his breath coming in choppy pants as he thrust into her over and over. "You make me…burn."

He buried his face in her hair and his mouth did sinful things to the side of her neck. Impossibly, he brought her even higher and higher, her every nerve ending centered on where they were joined.

The first fluttering of her climax began deep in her belly. She strained against him and he clamped his mouth down on hers, ravenous, devouring her whimpers as he pumped into her so deeply she cried out and exploded around him. He thrust again, once, twice, his entire body stiffening against her as his own climax claimed him.

He collapsed on top of her, crushing her into the mattress. But she didn't mind. They could have lain there forever with their limbs entwined and she wouldn't have ever wanted to move—except that she couldn't breathe.

"Dillon, I can't catch my breath."

"Me, either. You wore me out."

"Dillon!"

He laughed and pushed himself up on his forearms. He gave her a sleepy kiss, then flopped onto his back. "That was…"

"Incredible?"

"Amazing. Hot. Mind-blowing."

"Mind-blowing? Really?"

"Really," he mumbled, sounding as if he were drugged. "Now scoot over here and let's get some sleep."

She snuggled up against him, feeling content, secure.

"I can honestly say you're the best thing that's happened to me since I came to Destiny."

He chuckled and rubbed his hand up and down her bare back. "Considering everything that's happened to you so far, I'm not sure that's a compliment."

"Oh, it is. Before you, I could count on one hand the things I liked about small towns. I grew up in one. Without much to do except explore caves in the woods or make mazes in cornfields. I detest everything about them." She shivered dramatically. "Everything except you, of course. When I go back to Nashville you're the one memory I'll treasure from my time here."

His hand stilled on her back. "What exactly do you detest about small towns?"

She drew small circles in the light matting of hair on his chest. "The way everyone knows your business. I couldn't stand the lack of privacy, and the way gossip spreads so fast. In the city, I can do whatever I want and no one cares."

"Sounds like a lonely way to live."

"I have friends. They just don't butt into my personal business, or tell my parents every time I sneeze." She yawned and closed her eyes, drifting off to sleep with a smile on her face.

DILLON LAY AWAKE long after Ashley's deep breathing turned into soft snores. For a few minutes after loving her, he'd held an idyllic picture in his head, of Ashley staying in Destiny with him and exploring the attraction between them long after this case was resolved.

For a moment he'd forgotten how fragile life was, and how long it had taken him to climb out of the dark pit he'd fallen into after his sister died. He'd barely survived her loss, and knew that it would be agony experiencing that type of loss again when his parents eventually died, or his friends. There was nothing he could do to protect himself against that kind of hurt from the people he already knew, but he'd vowed not to let anyone else close enough to him to make him even more vulnerable.

Until he'd met Ashley, he'd kept his romantic relationships casual, without any promises or hope for something deep and lasting. He preferred it that way. But then he'd held Ashley in his arms and experienced a soul-shattering closeness he'd never felt with any other lover. And suddenly he was thinking about the long-term possibilities of a life he'd never dreamed he'd want.

But that brief glimpse of forever was now a bitter taste in his mouth. He and Ashley didn't want the same things in life. That was clear. He treasured living in a small town, and she despised that type of life. What she thought of as lack of privacy, he thought of as caring and concern. Everyone in Destiny was family to him, and he couldn't imagine any other kind of life.

He sighed and feathered his hands across her satiny-smooth skin, imprinting the way she felt against him in his memory, because he knew he'd never hold her like this again.

Chapter Twelve

After using the walkie-talkie to talk to Chris early the next morning to update him on their theory about Lauren Wilkes, Dillon led Ashley out on horseback before the sun came up. He told her it was because he didn't want to stay in one place too long, in case Iceman was actively looking for her. But really, he didn't expect anyone to find them up in the foothills of the Smokies, not this far from the farm. On horseback he had an excuse not to talk to her. Because really, what else was there to say?

His plan was to head southeast toward Walland because there was plenty of tree cover that way and when that thinned out, more cornfields to hide in. Once they put enough distance between them and Destiny, he'd call in a favor and have another friend put them up somewhere. Hopefully by then Chris would have convinced Special Agent Kent that Ashley wasn't guilty, and he would have found the evidence to corroborate their theory. Even better, if they caught Iceman by then, Ashley would be safe and could do what she wanted most.

To go home, leaving Destiny, and Dillon, far behind.

He turned in the saddle to check on her. But as expected she was hot on his tail, easily keeping up. She was an expert horsewoman. Too bad she'd decided to give up that part of her life. He couldn't imagine a life without horses in it. Riding was relaxing, a way to get away from anything bothering him. And sometimes, if he rode long enough and hard enough, he could almost escape the past.

The sound of hooves clattering against stones echoed up ahead. Dillon swore and clawed for his gun, but he was too late. The silhouette of a man sitting on a horse, aiming a rifle directly at him, sat squarely in their way, fifty yards ahead.

Dillon hauled back on the reins and turned his stallion sideways to block Ashley. Her mare hop-skipped to a stop right behind him.

"Hands up where I can see them," the man up ahead called out, his face still in shadow with the sun behind him.

"What do we do now?" Ashley whispered, holding her hands up.

"I'll let you know once I figure that out." He swore again and held his hands up in the air.

"Toss the gun," the man yelled.

Dillon hesitated.

The man in shadows jerked his gun up toward the sky and the bark of the rifle filled the air.

Dillon's stallion reared up and snorted, violently tossing his head, trying to get the bit between his teeth, fighting the reins. Dillon spoke to the horse in low tones to settle him down, and glanced back at Ashley. Her mare's eyes rolled white with fear but Ashley was keeping her under control.

"Toss the gun," the man repeated.

This time Dillon didn't hesitate. He removed the clip from his pistol and ejected the loaded round before tossing it into the bushes so it wouldn't accidentally fire when he threw it down.

"All right. The gun is gone. What do you want, Kennedy?"

"I'm not Kennedy."

The man urged his horse forward and tilted the rifle so it was pointing up at the sky. As his face passed from shadow to light, Dillon let loose a string of curses his mother would have tanned his hide over. Ashley's reaction was a bit less dramatic, but her gasp of surprise was loud enough for him to hear it. But when another figure rode out of the shadows, Dillon cursed even harder.

"*Et tu, Brute?* Did he happen to give you thirty pieces of silver, too?"

"I think you're mixing metaphors," Ashley whispered.

Dillon half turned in his saddle and gave her an incredulous look.

She shrugged. "Just saying."

He turned back around as Griffin and Special Agent Kent stopped a few feet away.

Griffin reddened. "Sorry, boss. He threatened to arrest me if I didn't help him track you up into the mountains."

Dillon sighed heavily. "It's okay. Forget it. Kent, what kind of dangerous game are you playing? Firing a gun around horses is asking for trouble."

"No game. I wanted to make sure I wouldn't get shot. That's what fugitives do when they're trapped. They shoot people."

Ashley urged her mare up beside Boomerang. "We're not fugitives," she said. "Dillon's on vacation and I'm a protected witness."

Dillon grinned. "Yeah. What she said."

"Now who's playing games?" Kent demanded. "That stunt you pulled back at the station only managed to put Miss Parrish in more danger. Kennedy is still out there somewhere and he's not the type to stop until he gets what he wants. You two need to come back with me right now so we can sort all this out."

"Why, so you can arrest me? Put me in jail for something I didn't do?" Ashley demanded.

"If putting you in jail will keep you safe, then yes. That's exactly what I'll do."

"Ashley isn't guilty," Dillon insisted. "Someone stole her identity, and we believe we know who that might be."

"Let me guess. Lauren Wilkes?"

"You knew?" Dillon demanded. "The whole time?"

"No. I suspected. But my suspicions were confirmed only a couple of hours ago. I've got an entire team looking into this case back in Knoxville and they haven't let up since day one. When they got a lead late yesterday that Wilkes might be involved, they stayed on it until they got proof. They called me and I knew I needed to find you, fast, and get Miss Parrish in protective custody."

"What kind of proof are you talking about?" Ashley asked, her voice shaky.

Dillon held his left hand out and she immediately entwined her fingers with his. Kent's gaze followed that action, his brows rising, but Dillon didn't care. Ashley had been through hell these past few days, and finding out her childhood friend had betrayed her so horribly had to be tearing her apart. If holding her hand helped her, so be it.

Griffin sat on his horse slightly back from Kent, his eyes wide with confusion.

"Griffin, go back to the farm," Dillon urged him. "Everything is okay. I'll call you later, all right?"

His face relaxed in relief. "Okay, Boss." A swift kick on the side of his horse and he was trotting back toward the farm.

"What kind of proof do you have against Lauren?" Ashley repeated, her voice impatient this time.

"We followed the money—some of it, anyway. We have bank security camera footage proving she used the Ashley Parrish identity to withdraw a large amount of money. Unfortunately, most of the money is still unaccounted for. We'd very much like to talk to Miss Wilkes, but she's disappeared."

"She went on a cruise to Jamaica."

Dillon squeezed her hand. "Honey, I think we both know she didn't. She's been lying to you for a long time."

Ashley's face fell and she looked away.

"So what's it going to take?" Kent asked. "Are you two coming back with me of your own free will, John Wayne and Daisy Duke? Or do I have to get a posse together?"

Dillon laughed. "You heard about that, huh?"

"Billy the Kid isn't very good at lying. He caved quicker than Griffin did."

"You can't find good help these days."

Kent smiled. "Now that you sent my trail guide away, I'm a bit at your mercy. How do we get back to town?"

"Going back to Harmony Haven is the shortest way."

"Lead on, then. I'll follow—"

A loud bang echoed through the trees.

Kent flew off his horse as if a battering ram had hit him in the side.

Ashley screamed.

"Go, go, go!" Dillon yelled. He slapped the mare's

rump, sending her at a full gallop into the cover of trees. He kicked his stallion and galloped after her just as another rifle boom exploded through the hills.

"We have to go back for him," Ashley yelled as she tried to pull her mare's reins out of Dillon's grip.

"He's dead. Stop fighting me. We have to get out of here." He maneuvered his horse over a fallen log, wincing when his arm felt as though it was about to come out of its socket from pulling the mare's reins behind him.

Ashley kicked her mare again, trying to pull the reins out of Dillon's hand. "You don't know that he's dead. We can't just leave him there. Oh, my God. Oh, my God."

Dillon jerked both horses to a stop. He'd finally realized there was no reasoning with Ashley right now. She was in hysterics. He couldn't blame her. She was in denial over what they'd both seen, and he wished he could somehow block the memory out, too. But it would be a long time before he forgot the sight of what that gunshot had done. No one could survive a shot like that to the head. He didn't need to turn around to confirm that.

His heart ached for the terror Ashley was feeling, but he couldn't take the time to try to soothe her. Iceman, or whoever had fired those shots, could catch up to them any second. Dillon leaned over and swept Ashley off her horse and into his arms. He settled her on his lap, draping her thighs over his, and wrapped one arm around her waist. He dropped the mare's reins, leaving her to find her own way back to the farm, and kicked the stallion into a fast canter through the woods.

It had been a couple of hours since Dillon had heard any sounds of pursuit, but it had also been hours since they'd seen any signs of civilization. His walkie-talkie was out of range to reach Chris, his phone had zero bars of service, and they were as deep into the mountains as he dared to go at this time of day. In a few more hours the sun would set, plunging even these foothills of the Smokies into much colder temperatures. With half their supplies gone with the mare, not to mention his gun, because Kent had made him toss it, they weren't prepared for staying the night up here. He had to get them out of the mountains and get help.

He turned his horse as close to due east as he could judge by the position of the sun and kicked him into a trot. Ashley didn't say anything. She hadn't spoken since he'd yanked her onto the saddle with him.

"Ashley," he whispered close to her ear, "I'm heading back toward town now. If I've got my bearings right, we'll end up right at my parents' farm. We can hunker down there and call for backup. We're going to be okay. Everything's going to be okay."

He waited, but when she didn't say anything, he sighed and leaned back.

She mumbled something.

He leaned back down. "What did you say?"

"We're going to your parents' house?"

"Yes. They're out of town, visiting—"

"Your brother. In Montana. I remember."

When she didn't say anything else, he straightened again. Relief swept through him that she was finally talking again, even if she wasn't saying much.

ASHLEY BLINKED AND looked down at Dillon's outstretched hands.

"Slide off the horse and I'll catch you."

Her mind was a fog and she felt as though she was waking from a horrible nightmare. Only she knew the nightmare was real. Special Agent Jason Kent had been murdered, brutally and horribly murdered, right in front of her. She shivered and looked around.

She was sitting on top of Dillon's stallion and he was standing below her, urging her to dismount. She surveyed where they were. They'd made it out of the foothills and were at the edge of another endless field of dried-up stalks of corn, ready for harvest. In the distance, the only sign of life was someone slowly driving an enormous combine in the middle of the field, perhaps two hundred yards away.

"Ashley, hurry. If Iceman's still on our trail, we're totally exposed now. We need to get out of his line of sight."

She mentally chastised herself for hesitating and putting him in danger. She immediately swung her leg over the back of the stallion. Dillon's hands came up around her waist and gently lowered her to her feet.

"I'm sorry. I know I totally checked out back there. I'm okay now."

He kissed her forehead. "Glad to have you back." He moved past her and yanked the duffel bag down from the back of the saddle. Then he loosely secured the reins around the horn and slapped the stallion's flank. The horse whinnied but didn't need further encouragement. He took off in a gallop back toward the foothills.

"Why did you let him go?"

"We're close to my parents' house now, just a hundred yards or so, at the end of the cornfield. I'm counting on Boomerang's training and homing instinct to get him back to Harmony Haven. That could buy us some time by creating another trail in the opposite direction from where we are."

He took her hand in his and tugged her into the edge

of the cornfield until the mountains fell away and all she could see was corn.

"I hope you're right, and Iceman follows the other trail."

"Me, too."

In a few minutes they emerged from the cornfield and climbed through the rails of a weathered gray wooden fence. A small gray-and-white wooden house perched fifty yards away, with graceful oaks leaning over it. A faded porch swing hung from a chain out front. An old tire moved in the breeze at the end of a rope hanging from one of the oak trees. And nestled a hundred yards behind the house was a pond with a little fountain in the middle.

"Reminds me of *my* parents' home, in Sweetwater. Minus the fountain," she said as they hurried to the front porch and paused at the door.

"Good memories?"

She hesitated, then smiled. "Yes. Good memories."

He ran his hand on top of the doorframe and pulled down a key and unlocked the door.

"I wouldn't dare keep a key there in the city," she said.

"I tell them all the time not to, but Dad's always losing his keys and Mom got tired of always calling me to come let them in. Half the windows are probably unlocked, too." He held the door open for her to enter the kitchen and locked the door behind them. "Call nine-one-one." He pointed to the phone hanging on the kitchen wall. "Tell them what happened to Special Agent Kent, and tell them to get a unit out to my parents' house. I'll check all the locks and get my father's gun."

"Wait, what's your parents' address?"

He grinned. "You don't need it. Everyone knows

where they live." He hurried through an archway into the adjacent family room.

Ashley made the call, her hands tightening around the phone as she watched him checking the sliding glass doors and windows in the next room before disappearing down a long, dark hallway.

When she hung up, she went down the hall and found a bathroom. She heard Dillon's footsteps upstairs. He was nothing if not thorough. She couldn't imagine anyone bothering to climb one of the oak trees surrounding the house to come in through one of the upstairs windows. But then again, after everything that had happened, she didn't mind him being extra careful.

She headed back into the family room, which boasted an eclectic mix of furnishings. An antique hutch filled with beautiful china sat next to a rather impressive collection of liquor bottles. She had to smile at that. A modern, dark brown leather recliner sat next to a worn couch with a faded blue floral pattern. The little decorative oak tables sprinkled around the room were covered with picture frames. But it was the mantel above the stone fireplace that held her attention. Her mother's collection of riding trophies was sparse in comparison to the awards marching across Dillon's parents' mantel.

She quickly realized there was organization to the chaos. The trophies on the left were mainly for football and all of them had the name Colton Gray on them, obviously Dillon's brother. In the middle were more football trophies and quite a few swim awards and ribbons with Dillon's name on them. That explained why he'd managed to swim through the storm-swollen river to save her on Cooper's Bluff.

When she checked out the last group of knickknacks,

she blinked in surprise. Horse-riding trophies competed with a healthy number of gymnastics awards. She read the name engraved on one of the little gold plates—Harmony Gray. So that was who the farm was named after, Dillon's sister. Ashley couldn't resist picking up a heart-shaped gold locket leaning against a plaque. She worked the delicate catch and opened it to reveal a picture of two young boys and a girl, obviously siblings, on the left side of the locket, and a picture of an older couple on the right that had to be Dillon's parents.

Dillon stepped into the room, his ever-present smile fading when he saw what she held.

Ashley had a feeling she'd just intruded into something private, but she couldn't stop herself from asking the obvious questions. "You have a sister named Harmony? You named your farm after her?"

He took the locket from her and set it back on the mantel, carefully adjusting the angle as if its exact placement mattered. When he looked back at her, there was none of the usual warmth in his expression and his eyes had turned cold. "*Had* a sister. Past tense."

He started to turn away but she put her arm on his, stopping him.

"Tell me about her."

"We don't have time."

His cold tone had her jerking her hand back.

He sighed heavily. "I'm sorry. It's just that…everyone around here knows about Harmony, so they don't ask, they never talk about her."

"I didn't mean to pry. Okay, maybe I did, a little. I was curious, but I didn't mean to open any old wounds."

He stared down at her, his expression softening. "I know. Come on. I'm going to get my dad's gun out of his safe."

They went back down the long hall into the last room on the right. A desk along the far wall held a sewing machine and an assortment of material and threads. Bolts of fabric lined racks on another wall.

"Your dad sews?" Ashley teased.

Dillon chuckled. "Not the last time I checked. Mom makes quilts and sells them to tourists at the flea market. She doesn't need the money, but since she's given nearly everyone in Destiny at least two quilts each over the years, she had to find someone else to give them to. Keeps her busy and happy."

He lowered himself to his knees on the tile floor in the middle of the room and pulled back a small rectangular rug to expose a trap door. He pulled it open to reveal a safe with a combination lock. The lock clicked and the safe opened. Dillon reached inside.

A whisper of sound had both of them turning around. Dillon threw his hands up just as Iceman swung one of the heavy trophies from the mantel at Dillon's head. Blood splattered from a gash in Dillon's scalp.

"Run, Ashley," he yelled as he warded off another crushing blow. The gun in his hand was useless, since it had a trigger lock and he hadn't had time to unlock it.

Ashley desperately looked around the room for something to use to help Dillon. But other than the sewing machine, which was too heavy to pick up, the hardest things in the room were the bolts of cloth.

Iceman swung the trophy again.

Dillon rolled out of the way just in time and Iceman fell to the ground. Dillon jumped to his feet and ran toward the other man, ready to tackle him. Iceman yanked a pistol out of his belt and pointed it up at Dillon's head, stopping him in his tracks.

The faint whine of sirens sounded in the distance.

"Looks like the cavalry is on their way." Iceman laughed. "Looks like they're too late." He steadied his gun.

Dillon lunged toward him.

The gun went off, sounding deafening in the small space.

Dillon fell to the floor, his eyes closed, blood pooling underneath his head.

Ashley screamed and dropped to her knees beside him. "Dillon, oh, my God, Dillon." She reached for him, but Iceman jerked her back. He grabbed her by her hair and dragged her out into the hall.

Ashley flailed her hands up, trying to stop the horrible burning pain in her scalp. She kicked her feet and tried to rake her nails down his arms. He stopped halfway down the hall and slapped her so hard she flew against the wall and fell to the floor.

She expected Iceman to backhand her again. When he didn't, she shoved her hair out of her eyes. The door to the antique hutch hung open, and Iceman stood in the middle of the family room pouring the contents of one of the bottles onto the area rug. The smell of alcohol hit her eyes, making them sting. What was he doing?

She braced her hands on the floor and wobbled to her feet.

A whoosh of heat and light had her flattening against the wall in shock. Oh, dear God, no. Iceman had set the rug on fire. The flames quickly moved to the couch and consumed the delicate cloth. Ashley turned and ran back down the hallway. If there was any chance Dillon was still alive, he was about to burn to death. She couldn't let that happen.

Rough hands closed around her waist and jerked her up into the air.

"No, let me go," she screamed.

Iceman ignored her struggles and ran with her down the hall, away from Dillon.

"You can't leave him here! He'll die!"

He threw her over his shoulder. When he reached the family room, he had to swerve back toward the fireplace to get around a chair that was on fire. Ashley flailed her hands out, trying to grab something to stop him, but all she managed to do was pull half the trophies off the mantel. Something small hit her hand and she grabbed it, her fingers closing around it as Iceman twisted and ran through the kitchen and outside. The back of a commercial-looking white van was a dark open maw. He pitched her like a sack of hay into the back and slammed the doors.

She cried out when her head slammed against the metal floor. She immediately pushed herself to her knees. When she saw what she'd grabbed off the mantel, she shoved it into her jeans pocket and scrambled toward the double doors at the back of the van. She jerked the handle. Nothing happened. She tried again, and again.

"Open the doors," she cried. "Please, you can't leave him in there! Dillon, Dillon!"

"It's no use. He locked it from the outside. There's no way out."

Ashley whirled around at the familiar-sounding voice just as the van took off, slamming her against the closed doors. She fell to the floor again and slammed her fist against the floor in frustration.

"I'm so sorry," the voice said again. "I never meant for this to happen. I'm so sorry, Ash."

She shoved her hair out of her face and looked into the tortured gaze of Lauren Wilkes.

Chapter Thirteen

Ashley blinked at Lauren, stunned to see her there. But when Lauren reached for her, Ashley shoved her out of the way and turned back to the doors. She put every ounce of strength she had into twisting and pulling at the handle. She fought the rocking motion of the van to keep her balance and slammed her body against the doors over and over. The doors didn't budge. The van kept barreling down the road.

And behind them, even though she couldn't see it, fire was greedily consuming the house where Dillon lay unconscious—or worse—on the floor.

A keening sound whistled between her teeth and she slid to the floor, her entire body racked with sobs.

Please, if there's any mercy in the world, let Dillon die before the fire reaches him. Please don't let him burn.

The sound of sirens rose loud in the air, closer, closer.

The van suddenly slowed, as if the driver didn't want to attract attention. Ashley didn't want the police to notice the van, either. If there was any hope of Dillon surviving, the police needed to reach the house as soon as possible.

Don't stop, don't stop. Keep going to the house!

One of her prayers was finally answered. The sirens didn't stop. Instead, they zoomed past, fading in the distance in the direction where the van had just come from.

"Ash?"

She drew great gulping breaths, then slowly straightened and leaned back against the side of the van and looked at her...friend? Enemy?

"Is it true?" she demanded. "Did you steal my identity and embezzle money?"

Lauren's gaze fell. "I...I was desperate. I couldn't pay the bills. I was about to be evicted. All I wanted was a chance to get some experience on my résumé, but my grades held me back. No one would hire me. It started out as one gig, just so I could eat. You have to understand. I didn't mean any harm."

"You didn't mean any harm? People have died! All because you were too proud to go home and ask your friends and family for help? Seriously? How many more people are going to die because of your selfishness?"

The stricken look on Lauren's face sent an automatic tug of guilt through Ashley, but she ruthlessly forced it away. Dillon didn't deserve to die because of Lauren's choices, and Lauren deserved no pity from her.

"I never... I didn't think anyone would get hurt or I never would have done it. It was so easy, and for the first time in my life I had money to buy nice clothes, go to dinner at a fancy restaurant, take trips. I know I was wrong, but it was like a snowball rolling downhill once it started. And then...I met David. We fell in love." A single tear ran down her cheek. "I was going to stop. We were going to run away together. And then they killed him." Her voice broke on a sob and she covered her face with her hands.

"David? Who's David?"

Lauren sniffled and wiped her tears. "David Dunlop. He was one of Todd Dunlop's sons. When I audited Dunlop Enterprises, I realized David was already taking money, so I…I threatened him, like I did the others, so he would give me some money. But he understood me like no one else ever has. His father was mean and cruel and made David beg for every cent even though his father was a billionaire. It was wrong how he treated David. We fell in love and made our plan, one big score and we'd get out. But his father grew suspicious and he sent Luther to investigate. Two days later, David died. The police said it was just a car crash, but Luther bragged about it to me, how he forced David off the road and he ran into a tree."

She wiped at her tears again. "Luther said I was next if I didn't give him the money David and I had taken." Her tear-bright gaze raised to Ashley's. "But I didn't have the account numbers or any way to access them. David was going to give me the account numbers, but he died before he could."

The van made another slow turn, as if the driver was making doubly sure no one would notice him or have any reason to be suspicious. It bounced and rocked on its springs, slowing even more as it made its way down what felt like a dirt road.

Lauren squeezed her hands together in her lap. "Ash, I'm so sorry. Luther threatened to kill me. You have to understand. I had to buy some time while I tried to figure a way out of this mess. I never dreamed that he would…" She squeezed her eyes shut and shook her head. "Please forgive me."

"Why do you keep apologizing to me?" The van stopped, its brakes squeaking.

A panicked look swept across Lauren's face.

"Where are we?" Ashley demanded. "What have you done?"

Lauren suddenly grabbed Ashley by the shoulders. "Listen to me. I told Luther you were in on everything with me. I told him that you had the access information for the accounts. He expects you to be able to wire the money to his account."

"What? Why? Why did you tell them that?"

Footsteps crunched outside. The mumble of low voices sounded through the door.

"You have to pretend you can access the account, Ash. You have to buy us some more time. If you can't bluff them, we're both going to die."

Ashley's stomach sank. Her mind raced, trying to absorb everything Lauren had said. What was she going to do?

A metallic noise sounded outside. The handle flipped down and the door jerked open.

Iceman stood in the opening, and he wasn't alone. Two men flanked him. All three of them wore large guns holstered on their hips. Behind the van, two more men sat in a forest-green sedan. And they were all staring at her.

"End of the road, ladies," Iceman growled. "Someone had better tell me how to get my money or you both die." He drew his gun and pointed it directly at Ashley. "I'm going to count to three, and then you either tell me what I need to know or I put a bullet in your brain."

No, no, no, what was she supposed to do?

"One."

Bile rose in her throat. She had to tell him how to get the money. But how could she do that? Only one person knew the account number and any access IDs and passwords that might be needed, and that person was dead.

She darted a glance at Lauren, but there was no help in that quarter. Lauren's eyes were closed and she was rocking back and forth, as if she'd given up and was waiting for a bullet.

"Two."

Oh, God. She had to do something. A computer. She needed a computer to buy them time, to pretend she knew how to access the accounts. But what if he had a computer with him? That would be too fast, too easy, and wouldn't buy her any time to find a way out. So what could she do?

"Three. Tell me what I want to know or I'm pulling the trigger."

"Okay, okay!" She held up her hands. "Put the gun away. Please. I'll tell you."

His eyes narrowed. "Tell me, and if I believe you, then I'll put the gun away." His finger flexed on the trigger.

"My computer," she gasped. "I need my computer."

"Use mine." He motioned to one of the other men, who headed toward the front of the van.

"No, no, that won't work. I have to have *my* computer."

He pressed the gun against her forehead. "Why?"

Why? Her mind went blank. All she could focus on was the cold feel of the barrel pressing against her skin.

"Because she has the access codes in a file," Lauren blurted out. "And they're encrypted. She has to run the file through special software on her laptop to decode them!"

Access codes? Encrypted? Decode? What was Lauren doing, trying to make it sound as though Ashley was some kind of genius corporate spy? She kept her face carefully blank, trying not to let her frustration show, hoping she could go along with Lauren's crazy lie and look convincing.

Iceman slowly lowered the gun and shoved it into the holster. "All right. Where's your computer?"

"I don't know," she whispered.

He reached for his gun.

"Wait, wait. I remember. I had it with me up in the mountains. It was in my duffel bag, the one..." She swallowed, trying to force words past the anguish tightening her throat. "It's in the bag...Dillon...tied behind the mare's saddle."

He narrowed his eyes at her. "I remember the mare. He let it go when you two raced off on the other horse." His hand relaxed away from his gun, as if her mentioning the mare had lent credibility to Lauren's made-up story. "Where's the mare now?"

She hesitated. Dillon had said the mare was trail trained, that she'd go right back home to the farm. But there were people at the farm—Griffin, the farmhands. She couldn't put them in danger by leading him there. All that would do was buy a few more minutes, or however long it would take to get to the farm. Once he realized she didn't have any special access codes, she was as good as dead anyway. She couldn't trade a few more minutes for the lives of innocent people.

"I don't know."

He whipped his gun out and pressed it against her forehead again. "Rethink that answer."

She swallowed hard. "I don't know where the mare is."

He grabbed Lauren by the hair and yanked her to the opening at the back of the van. Lauren whimpered and grabbed his hands, blinking against the rush of tears that flowed down her cheeks. Iceman pressed the gun against her temple. "Tell me where the mare is, or she dies."

"Ash, please," Lauren pleaded. "Please don't let me die."

"Hold it, wait!" she yelled, hating herself for the choice she was making, but she couldn't let him kill Lauren. She would just have to pray she could somehow do something to alert Griffin and the others before they fell prey to the Iceman. "The mare would have gone home. She should be at Dillon's horse farm by now, Harmony Haven."

He must have seen the truth in her eyes, because he shoved Lauren away and slammed the doors shut.

DILLON STARED UP at Chris, Donna and the chief and tried to make sense of why he was lying flat on his back on the grass and the three of them were on their knees, bending over him. Black smoke billowed into the blue sky above him and the acrid smell burned his nostrils and made his eyes water. Sirens sounded far off in the distance.

A violent cough racked his body and set his head to pounding as if a herd of horses were galloping around the inside of his skull. He cursed and raised his hand to cradle his head, but Chris grabbed his arm, stopping him.

"Be still, John Wayne. You're bleeding all over the place." As if to prove it, he held up what appeared to be a shirt. Dillon couldn't be sure, because it was covered in blood. Chris turned it and pressed it back against the side of Dillon's head.

Dillon sucked in a breath at the sharp pain that lanced through his skull. "What happened, Billy Bob?" he asked, his voice coming out a thick rasp.

Chris exchanged a surprised glance with the others. "It's Billy the Kid. Get it right, partner. And as for what happened, we were hoping you would tell us that."

The chief squatted down beside him. "Miss Parrish called nine-one-one. She explained that Luther Kennedy murdered Special Agent Kent and you two were holed up in your parents' house and needed backup. When we got here, half the house was on fire and the rest of it was full of smoke. Chris, fool that he is, raced inside. Lucky for you, he found you and got you out in time." He cleared his throat and looked away, as if he couldn't bring himself to say the rest.

"What?" Dillon demanded. His stomach knotted and his heart slammed in his chest as the sickening realization hit him. He didn't see Ashley anywhere. He grabbed the chief's arm. "What happened to her? Tell me!"

Chris pulled the shirt away from the side of Dillon's head as if to inspect the cut, then shook his head and pressed the shirt back. "The fire was too intense. I barely got you out before the rest of the house went up. If Miss Parrish was inside…" He shook his head. "I'm sorry, man. We got here too late."

Images slammed into him. Ashley beside him in his mother's sewing room, watching him open the floor safe. Movement out of the corner of his eye. Too late, he saw Iceman, swinging one of those damn swim trophies at him. Ashley screaming, trying once again to help him instead of running to safety like she should have. A deep, burning pain in the side of his head. Falling to the floor. Pain shooting through his head, making everything foggy. Unable to move even as he heard Ashley scream and he realized Iceman was taking her away. Then nothing, until now.

He tried to sit up, but Chris and Donna both pushed him back down.

"For God's sake, Dillon," Donna chastised him. "You've got lumps the size of Ping-Pong balls all over your head. And if I'm not mistaken, a bullet grazed your scalp. You've probably got a concussion, and if you get up you'll start bleeding again. Lie down and wait for the ambulance."

Dillon shoved Chris's hand away. "Iceman has Ashley. I remember him pulling her down the hall. He has her. I have to help her."

"What makes you think he didn't kill her and leave her in the house?" the chief asked.

"He could have killed her several times over already, but each time he didn't. He wants her alive. Whatever he wants her for, he still hasn't gotten it. He took her. He's got her. Let me up, Chris. Or I'm going to knock some teeth out."

Chris frowned but pulled his hands back.

Dillon scrambled to his feet, then wobbled as the world tilted and spun around him.

Chris swore and grabbed his arm, steadying him.

Dillon drew several deep breaths and the spinning stopped. For the first time he realized exactly where he was—the edge of the front lawn of his parents' house, or what was left of it. Flames still ate at the wooden structure, but the second floor wasn't even recognizable anymore. His chest tightened and for a moment he couldn't seem to draw a breath. All those memories, his mother's quilts, the trophies she'd treasured…all gone, including Harmony's. He dropped his head to his chest. He just couldn't watch his parents' dreams going up in smoke anymore.

And that's when he saw them.

He bent down, studying the dirt where the yard ended and the road began. "Fresh tire tracks. Wide apart. And he must have turned the wheel right here," he said, pointing. "That marks the wheelbase, longer than a car. Iceman took Ashley away in a small truck or a van of some kind. Did you pass any vehicles on the road when you came here?"

Chris shook his head. "No. This isn't exactly a high-traffic area around here. I suppose he could have gone down a side road if he heard our siren."

"Since there's not much traffic, that should make figuring out what he was driving and where it went fairly easy," Dillon said.

The sirens were much louder now. Lights flashed on an ambulance about a half mile down the road, racing toward the house. Behind it, a tanker truck turned onto the long road.

The chief stepped closer, as if to make sure he could be heard over the noise. "I bet if we make a few phone calls we'll pinpoint exactly what type of vehicle drove through here and we'll be able to track it at least until it reaches a major highway, if that's where Iceman… Luther went."

"I'm on it." Donna took out her cell phone.

Five minutes later, Dillon was sitting on a gurney in the back of the ambulance having his head sewn up. He refused to go to the hospital until Ashley was found, but he'd compromised and agreed to a quick repair while Donna worked on figuring out exactly where Iceman's vehicle—which she'd determined from eyewitnesses on the road was a white panel van—had gone.

Firemen worked to put out the blaze, even though Dillon didn't see the point anymore. The house was a total loss.

"Let's talk it out," Dillon said, not willing to put all his hopes on Donna being able to figure out where the van went. "Maybe we can figure out where Iceman would take Ashley and why. What did you find out while we were holed up in the mountains?"

"Random stuff," Chris said. "We don't have much."

"Start with the Dunlop family and their business. What do you know about them?"

"Okay. Todd Dunlop had three kids, a girl and two boys. They're all grown adults now. Patricia Dunlop, the woman who came to the station, is his third wife."

"You mean Cruella de Vil's not related to any of the children?"

"No. Why?"

"Just thinking out loud. What else, what else?" He winced when the EMT pressed gauze against his head.

"They had a prenup agreement, so if anything happened to the husband, the wife got nothing."

"What about life insurance?"

"Everything is going to charity. The wife, the kids, they don't get anything."

Dillon stared at Chris. "Nothing? He was a billionaire and he didn't provide for his family upon his death?"

"Not that we've been able to tell. The family plans to ask for an injunction while they fight in the courts. But what difference does it make? Todd Dunlop wasn't murdered."

"I know, I know. I'm trying to figure out how Iceman, Luther Kennedy, fits into all of this and why he wants Ashley alive. We know he was a thug, but that Todd Dunlop trusted him. Why would he trust a shady guy like that?"

The chief hooked his fingers into his belt loops.

"Maybe he was afraid of Luther. Maybe Luther blackmailed him into giving him a job."

Dillon glanced at Chris. "Any evidence of that?"

"No. None."

Donna ended her latest call and joined them. "I've got a call tree going like wildfire. If anyone knows anything, they'll let us know."

Dillon nodded his thanks. "We need more information on Luther. Donna, would you place a call to the Knoxville FBI office? Don't tell them about Kent yet. That will bog down the conversation and we don't have time for that right now. Tell them Kent is unavailable and we need everything they have on Luther right away."

"You got it." She pulled her phone out again.

The EMT finished bandaging the side of Dillon's head. "I highly recommend you go to the hospital, sir. You might have a concussion."

"I'll go later."

The EMT glanced at the chief.

The chief sighed and nodded. "Go on back to town. He's not going to change his mind right now."

Dillon eased himself off the gurney and out of the ambulance and stood with Chris and the chief as the ambulance headed back up the road. "Todd Dunlop essentially committed suicide by cop at Gibson and Gibson. He wanted to kill the person he felt was responsible for embezzling funds and ruining his company. Before Kent was killed, he told me he had evidence that indicated Lauren Wilkes, Ashley's best friend, was the one who stole her identity. By Ashley's own admission, her friend wasn't that good as an auditor, barely even passed her classes. That reinforces Kent's theory that Lauren teamed up with people at the companies to get them to embezzle in some kind of blackmail scheme.

What we need to know is who she teamed up with at Dunlop Enterprises."

Chris frowned. "But we already know—Luther embezzled the money."

"Are we positive?"

The chief shook his head. "It seems the most likely scenario, but no, I haven't seen any real proof yet."

"I don't think he did," Dillon said.

"Why not?" Chris asked.

"Because Luther is so determined to keep Ashley alive. He doesn't strike me as the type to go after someone that hard unless there's a benefit to him. And he's taking tons of risks—shooting at cops, killing a federal agent. If he's got millions stashed away, why not take the money and run? Why risk being killed or sent to prison?"

Chris shook his head. "Son of a… He doesn't have the money. That's the *only* reason he would take those risks."

"I agree," Dillon said. "Somehow, abducting Ashley is the key to him getting the money. We know he had it at one time, or at least access to the money. If he was partnering with Lauren Wilkes to embezzle the money, she was the only one with access to it. Somehow she has the money and he can't get to it. And he believes Ashley is his key to getting the money."

"Lauren Wilkes is the key," the chief said. "Find Lauren—"

"And we find Ashley," Dillon finished.

The chief folded his arms. "We still don't know Miss Parrish's role in this. Maybe she was colluding with her friend in the embezzlement."

Dillon gritted his teeth. "No. She wouldn't do that."

"You sure about that? Willing to bet your life on that?"

"Yes." And suddenly, he knew it was true. He trusted Ashley, with no reservations. "I'm not sure why I'm so sure, but I am."

Donna hung up her cell phone again. "You're not going to believe this." She joined their circle by the road. "Luther Kennedy wasn't just an errand boy for Todd Dunlop. Luther was Todd's illegitimate son. And that's not all. Interviews with the Dunlops' household staff indicate the marriage was on rocky ground and that Patricia Dunlop had contacted a lawyer about breaking the prenuptial agreement. She was told it was rock solid, no chance that it could be broken." Her face broke into a wide smile. "Ask me what else I found out."

"We don't have time to make guesses," Dillon said.

Her smile dimmed. "Okay, okay. With the Dunlop family being billionaires, their children's escapades tended to catch media attention. Which means a lot of their actions get caught on camera by paparazzi. And one of those camera hounds snapped pictures of one of the sons, David, with his latest girlfriend, about a month before Todd Dunlop's death. Guess who she was?"

Dillon stared at her. "Lauren Wilkes?"

"Yep. And guess who was killed in a car accident, a one-vehicle accident with no witnesses, a few days before the Gibson and Gibson shooting?"

Chris, Dillon and the chief all exchanged glances. "David Dunlop," they said in unison.

"Yep." Donna looked very pleased with herself.

"So what the heck is going on?" Dillon scrubbed the stubble on his jaw. "Did David know about the embezzlement? Do we have a love triangle here? Lauren played Luther and David against each other and tried to skip town with the money? And Luther killed David?"

"It all comes back to the money," the chief said. "But I still don't understand how it all fits together."

Donna's phone rang. She grabbed it while all eyes focused on her. "Yep, yep, right. Got it. Thanks." She hung up, her mouth flattening into a tight line. "I was able to confirm sightings of the van up to the Youngbloods' farm ten minutes west of here as the crow flies. But I haven't gotten anything after that. I'm sorry, Dillon."

Dillon gritted his teeth and gave her a crisp nod.

The chief gave him a sympathetic look. "Donna and I will go back to town. I'll get everyone looking into this case whether they're a detective or not. We'll find out everything there is to know about Luther Kennedy. We'll figure out where he went. Chris, take Dillon to the hospital to get checked out."

"I don't need to go to the hosp—"

"That's an order, Detective Gray. An order you had better follow this time." He motioned to Donna and they got in his car and headed down the road.

"Come on," Chris said. "As soon as the doctor checks you out, I'll take you back to the station so you can help with the investigation."

Without a word, Dillon swung himself up into the passenger seat of his friend's four-wheel-drive pickup. But when the truck reached the end of the road and Chris was about to turn right toward town, Dillon grabbed the steering wheel.

"Turn left," Dillon ordered.

"Left? Why?"

"Because that's the way to the Youngbloods' farm."

"No way. You heard the chief."

"Fine. I'll hitch a ride or steal a car, whatever it takes. But I'm not going back to town when I know Luther has

Ashley, and he drove west." He jerked the door handle and opened the door.

Chris grabbed his arm. "Hold it, hold it." He sighed heavily. "I guess I can always drive a tractor for a living if the chief fires me. Shut the dang door."

As soon as Dillon shut the door, Chris wheeled the truck west and floored the accelerator.

Chapter Fourteen

A short, bumpy ride later, the van jerked to a stop, its brakes squealing in protest. Lauren grabbed Ashley's hand, her terror-filled gaze latching onto hers.

It hurt Ashley even to look at the woman she'd grown up with, knowing all the death her selfishness had caused. But Ashley also knew the next few minutes might be their last. She didn't want to die with all this anger and resentment inside. She closed her fingers around Lauren's and squeezed, giving her a small smile of encouragement.

Shoes crunched on gravel, coming around both sides of the van toward the back.

"We can't outfight these men," Ashley whispered. "Our only chance is to drag this out as long as we can. Hopefully the police are looking for us. It's our job to outsmart these guys and buy the police the time they need. Or until we can figure out a way to escape. Okay?"

Before Lauren could answer, the doors jerked open. Iceman stood in the middle, flanked by his two thugs. He drew his gun and pointed it at Ashley.

"You. Out. The other one stays here."

Lauren's hand squeezed painfully tight around Ashley's, and Ashley knew exactly why. The man on

Iceman's left side had a predatory gleam in his eye as he stared at Lauren, as if he had plans for her.

"No, I can't do this alone. I need her help," Ashley stammered out.

Iceman's eyes narrowed. "You said you have the codes on your computer."

"Yes, yes, I know. But Lauren and I are a team. We each know different parts of the…encryption algorithm. We set it up that way so neither of us could take all the money ourselves. Both of us have to work together."

Greed and lack of trust were apparently things Iceman identified with. Some of his own distrust faded and he stepped back. "All right. Both of you. Get out."

The man who'd been staring at Lauren gave Iceman a sullen look.

"Later," Iceman said in a low tone as if he didn't think either of the women understood that he was promising Lauren to the other man.

A shiver ran through Lauren, transmitting to Ashley through their joined hands. They climbed out of the van, which was parked beside Dillon's big white house. Her last memories of him, lying on the floor, blood pooling around his head, had her throat closing up.

Iceman's gun shoved against her back. "Move. To the barn out back. Let's find this mare of yours and get that computer."

DILLON SHOOK THE man's hand and turned with Chris to head back to the truck parked in the man's driveway. Mr. Jones had only recently moved to Destiny and he'd been in town buying groceries until a few minutes earlier. He didn't know anything about a white van in the area. And from the way his eyes had grown big and round as he noted Dillon's bloodstained hair and shirt and Chris's soot-streaked face, Dillon was betting the man might be rethinking his decision to move here.

Chris pulled back out onto the rural two-lane highway. They'd stopped at half a dozen homes already and either the people weren't home or they hadn't noticed a van drive by. But he wasn't giving up yet. Someone had to have seen Iceman.

The cell phone holstered on Dillon's hip buzzed, letting him know he had a text.

Chris slanted him a look as he pulled the phone out. "Did the chief realize we aren't on our way into town and he's firing us both by text?"

A familiar canned message filled the screen. "It's my home security system. One of Mr. Finley's cows probably escaped again." He punched the attached picture icon. A white van filled the screen.

With Iceman at the wheel.

And behind it was another car, with two more men inside.

"Turn around, turn around. Iceman's at Harmony Haven." They'd passed his driveway ten minutes earlier.

Chris slowed and turned around in the middle of the highway. "What's he want at your house?"

"I have no idea. But he brought muscle with him. I count five guys total—three in the front of the van and two in a car following. No telling how many might be in the back of the van, though." He punched another button on his phone and put the call on speaker so Chris could hear it, too.

"Last I heard," Chief Thornton's voice came through the phone, "they don't allow people to use cell phones in the emergency room. I had better hear a nurse telling you to hang up or I'm going to be royally ticked off that you aren't where I told you to be."

"My security alarm just snapped a picture of Iceman and at least four other men heading down my driveway."

"What the heck is he going to your house for?"

Chris slowed and turned onto the long road that led to the house.

"I don't know," Dillon said. "But you need to activate the SWAT team and get them over here."

"Here? Here? Are you telling me you and Downing are at your house instead of the hospital?" The chief added a few choice swear words, not waiting for a response. "When this is over, if we all live to tell about it, I'm going to make you scrub my executive bathroom for an entire year until you learn to respect the chain of command. You got that, Gray?"

Chris laughed.

Dillon narrowed his eyes. "Yes, sir. Got it. Sir, the SWAT team—"

"Yeah, yeah. They're gearing up right now. Let me talk to Downing."

Dillon held the phone closer to Chris but left it on speaker.

"This is Downing, sir."

"The team will be there in twenty minutes. We'll bring your gear. I don't care if you have to sit on Detective Gray or handcuff him to the bumper. Do not, under any circumstances, let him go after this Iceman on his own. That's an order. If you're not both waiting for us when we get there, you can kiss your jobs goodbye. By the time I bad-mouth you all over the county, you'll be lucky if you can get a job as a door greeter at Walmart. You got that?"

Chris winced. "Yes, sir. Loud and clear. Wait for backup."

Dillon ended the call and shoved the phone back in its holster.

Chris pulled the truck to the shoulder and cut the engine. "I don't suppose there's any way to convince you to wait like Thornton ordered?"

"Not in this lifetime. And if you try to handcuff me to the bumper, I'm going to fight like hell."

"Yeah, I figured that."

"There's no need for you to get in trouble with me. Give me your gun and wait here for the team."

"Shut up and pop the glove box open."

Dillon opened the glove box and grinned. "Does this mean what I think it means?"

"I reckon I can get used to saying 'Welcome to Walmart.' Kind of has a nice ring to it."

Dillon grabbed the Glock 17 out of the glove box and they both hopped out of the truck.

ICEMAN GRABBED ASHLEY'S arm at the entrance to the barn. "If we see anyone, you'd better convince them nothing's wrong and find that computer." He shoved the gun against the side of her ribs as if to remind her it was there.

She nodded. He motioned for two of the men, the ones who'd been in the car, to accompany him and Ashley inside. The others waited outside with Lauren.

"I can have my gun out in less than a second. And there are two more gunmen behind me. Remember that." He shoved his gun in his waistband at the small of his back. "Open the door."

Ashley grabbed the handle and pulled the door back on its rails as she'd seen Dillon do the day before. She stepped inside the barn, blinking until her eyes adjusted to the darkened interior.

Griffin stood in the middle of the aisle, a scrub brush in one hand and a bucket of water in the other. His brows raised in surprise. "Miss Parrish. I figured you and the boss were still at the police station. The FBI man, he let you go?"

At his mention of Special Agent Kent, Ashley closed her eyes, horrible images flashing across the inside of her lids, images of the agent being swept off his saddle by the force of a rifleman's bullet.

Iceman nudged her. "The computer," he whispered.

She opened her eyes and saw that Griffin was frowning now, his gaze jumping from her to the man beside her, then to the others a few feet farther back. She forced her lips into what she hoped was a reassuring smile, her only goal to get Griffin to leave without becoming suspicious, so he wouldn't get hurt.

"Mr. Griffin, good to see you again. Actually, ah, Dillon is still…at the police station. He sent me—us—back for my computer. It was in the duffel bag on the back of the mare. Dillon said she'd follow the trail back to the farm. Have you seen her?"

He nodded slowly, his gaze staying on Iceman. "Yes. She's in her stall. Came back about an hour ago, along with the boss's stallion. Both of the duffel bags are in the tack room." He set the bucket and brush down beside one of the stalls. "I'll get them for you. Why don't you have your gentleman friend wait here and you can help me find it."

"Okay, thanks." She started forward, but Iceman grabbed her arm.

His gun was out in a flash and he shoved it against Ashley's side. "Hold it. We'll all get the bags together."

She winced at the feel of the cold metal shoving against her ribs. Griffin waited for them to reach him, then he slowly turned and they headed into the tack room. The two bags were sitting on top of a trunk beneath a row of harnesses.

"Stop," Iceman ordered.

Griffin looked at him in question.

"Miss Parrish will get what she needs."

Ashley hurried forward and retrieved her computer bag. Her purse was right next to it, and she knew her cell phone was inside. But there was no way to unzip the purse and get her phone without Iceman seeing. She glanced over at Griffin, then at the duffel, trying to signal him in case he could get to her purse later.

"You've got the computer now. Get over here. And you'd better not be bluffing about being able to log in and get my money out of that account."

Dread settled into the pit of her stomach like a block of ice. She hurried out of the tack room. Iceman backed up, hauling her against his side. She noticed he winced when he did so, which reminded her that she'd shot him—or at least she thought she had—in the shoulder back on Cooper's Bluff. The injury must not have been as bad as she'd thought, because he was using his arm just fine. But that little telltale wince told her it at least pained him. That was something she'd file away in case she could use it to her advantage.

"You," he said, motioning to Griffin with his gun. "How many workers are on the farm right now?"

"None. It's just me."

The deafening sound of the gun being fired filled the barn.

Griffin collapsed to the ground, holding his thigh.

Ashley gasped and started forward to help him, but Iceman jerked her back again.

"He'll live, unless he does something stupid. Like

lie to me again. I repeat. How many others are on the farm right now?"

"Four," he gasped through clenched teeth. "They're out riding the fence line, checking for breaks."

"Call them back here, now. You do anything to warn them and the next bullet goes in your brain."

Griffin kept one hand pressed against the wound on his thigh and used his other hand to pull out his cell phone. His face was pale and drawn as he punched in a number and made the first call.

A few minutes later, Griffin and the farmhands were locked in the tack room. Iceman had taken all their cell phones, ensuring they had no way to call for help. But he hadn't taken the one from Ashley's purse. She prayed Griffin or one of the others would realize that before it was too late.

One of Iceman's men kicked out some planks from a stall and used them to brace the tack room door closed, effectively sealing Griffin and his men inside.

"Stay here and keep a watch out," he instructed the three men. "If anyone approaches the house or the barn, shoot them." He led Ashley out of the barn toward the house, with Lauren and her bodyguard pulling up the rear.

DILLON AND CHRIS stayed off the road and made their way through the woods toward the house. When they reached the top of the last hill that looked down on Dillon's property, they both paused.

"Too bad we don't have any binoculars." Dillon braced his hand against the tree beside him. "I don't know if we're dealing with five men or more, or whether they're in the house or one of the outbuildings."

"Or both," Chris added.

"Yeah, or both."

"That backup is sounding really good about now." Chris looked at his watch. "The team should be here in another ten minutes."

"Ashley could be dead in ten minutes. I can't wait that long." He didn't say what they were both thinking, that she could already be dead.

"You have a plan?" Chris asked.

"Working on it." He studied his property with fresh eyes, not as the owner, but as a man who needed to sneak down the hill and into the house without being seen. There weren't any shrubs up close to the house, by design. No sheltering trees close enough to take cover behind, or to enable someone to climb into an upstairs window. Thirty head of horses grazed all over the green pastures but again, no cover. The only cover was the cornfield, but that was behind and to the right of the house, with no way to get to it without being seen, unless they went back out to the main road again and worked their way from the east side of his neighbor's property.

"I've got to hand it to you," Chris said. "You built this place like a fortress. No one's getting close to it without being seen."

"Tell me about it. Looks like we've got two choices. Either we go back out and work our way through the cornfield, which will take a good twenty minutes or more, or we take our chances, hope no one's watching, and make a run for it."

"I vote for the cornfield."

"I vote for making a run for it."

"That could be suicide," Chris said.

"We've both got vests on."

"What if they take a head shot?"

"Yeah, well, that would suck."

His cell phone vibrated again. "Maybe our backup is already here." He pulled the phone out, but it wasn't a text message this time. And he recognized the number that was calling him. He shot Chris a surprised glance and answered the call. "Ashley? Where are you?"

"It's Griffin, boss. I'm using Miss Parrish's phone. She's in trouble, sir."

The relief that had shot through him when he thought she was calling turned to a bitter taste in his mouth. "Tell me what's going on." He listened to Griffin's tale, his stomach tightening with dread. "All right. We'll get you and your men out. Hang tight." He shoved the phone back in its holder.

"What's going on?" Chris asked.

"Griffin confirmed Iceman's got Ashley with him. Iceman shot Griffin in the leg and locked him and the farmhands in the tack room in the barn. He said Iceman seems to expect Ashley to use her computer to log into an account and get his money. That's why he came here, to get her computer."

"But she's not the one who embezzled the money. Her friend did. So why isn't Iceman having Lauren log into the account?"

"I don't know. All I do know is that once Ashley isn't able to log in, she's in real trouble."

"What are we going to do?"

Dillon looked out over the fields again, a kernel of an idea popping into his head. "How much longer before SWAT gets here?"

"Five minutes, give or take."

He explained his idea.

"You're crazy. Just wait and we'll do the cornfield approach. It's the only safe way to get to the house."

"You heard what Griffin said. I've got to buy Ashley

some time. And I can't leave Griffin and his men there to die if Iceman decides to eliminate witnesses. Are you going to stand there arguing with me or are you going to help?"

He swore. "Fine. Do it. I'll intercept SWAT and tell them your idiotic plan. Dillon—" Chris put his hand on his shoulder "—don't make me have to put on a suit. I don't even dress up for church. I sure don't want to dress up for a funeral."

Dillon grinned. "You want me to be careful and don't get killed. Got it." He melted back into the trees and headed along the tree line, away from the house.

Chapter Fifteen

Dillon stopped his mad dash through the woods. He was as close to the wooden rail fence that bordered the pasture as he was going to get without stepping into the open. Hopefully, he'd have a little luck on his side. He was going to need it.

He put his fingers in his mouth and let out a shrill whistle. Moments later he heard the sound of hooves drumming against the ground, getting louder and louder. Boomerang topped the far hill and headed straight for the fence. He hop-skipped to a halt right before running into the fence and dipped his nose over the top rail in question, his nostrils flaring as he snorted a welcome.

Dillon glanced back toward the house, a hundred yards away. He didn't see anyone, but that didn't mean they couldn't see him once he left the cover of trees. He took off, sprinted to the fence, then used the bottom rail to boost himself up and onto the stallion's back.

Boomerang snorted and danced away from the fence.

"Easy, boy, easy." Dillon sat high on the withers, like a jockey getting ready for a race, and got a good handful of mane in his right hand to hold on to. He leaned as far to the left as he dared, using his legs to guide the horse and keeping his head and shoulders hidden by the long-flowing mane and the horse's thick neck. "Come on, Boomerang. Let's round up some help." He squeezed his legs and guided the stallion across the field toward a group of trail-trained horses, the kind that would docilely follow Dillon's lead.

ICEMAN SHOVED ASHLEY and Lauren into Dillon's library and paused in the doorway to speak to one of his thugs. Ashley stumbled and had to catch herself on the table in the middle of the room, the same table where Dillon and his fellow detectives had been reviewing the case notes two nights ago. A pang of sadness went through her and she glanced around the room as if she could somehow bring Dillon back just by picturing him here. Her gaze swept past the bookshelves, the bank of TV screens to the windows… Her gaze shot back to the TV screens and her mouth dropped open.

It couldn't be, could it?

There, on the bottom screen, the security camera showed a view of the northwest pasture. A group of six horses trotted through the field, and on the neck of the bay-colored stallion leading the pack clung a familiar figure—Dillon.

Ashley gasped and hurried farther into the room. She glanced back. Iceman was still in conversation with the other man in the doorway. Lauren stood beside the table, watching Ashley with a look of confusion on her face. Ashley grabbed a book from one of the nearby bookshelves and quickly dragged one of the ladder-back chairs over to the corner, praying the chair would block the TV screen from view. She plopped down and opened the book just as Iceman looked over at her.

He frowned. "Put the book down and sit at the table. Get on the computer and access that account. Now."

She got up, left the book on the seat and hurried over to the table. She sat as far away from the TVs as she could, hoping to keep Iceman from noticing the screens.

Lauren sat beside her and placed the laptop on the table. "What are you doing?" she whispered.

Ashley kept a wary eye on Iceman, who'd gone back to the doorway and was talking to the other gunman again.

"Dillon's alive," she whispered. "I saw him on that bottom screen."

"Dillon? The hot SWAT guy you told me about on the phone?" Lauren whispered back.

"Yes. I thought he was killed in the fire, back at the house where Iceman grabbed me. But he's alive."

Lauren's brows rose. "Iceman?"

"Luther Kennedy."

"Oh." She scooted closer to Ashley. "Shouldn't we power up the computer and at least pretend to access the account?"

"You're right, but we need to figure out some way to stall Iceman." She turned the laptop on and once it booted up she used her Wi-Fi hotspot software to access the internet through a cell phone network. "Now what?" she whispered. "Any ideas?"

"Why don't you access your email? If he asks questions, you can tell him you hid the codes in one of the emails in your folders."

"Good idea. I haven't checked my email since before the shooting at Gibson and Gibson. I probably have tons." She glanced up to make sure Iceman wasn't listening before opening her email.

Lauren peered over her shoulder, her face so close to Ashley's that her breath tickled the fine hairs on Ashley's neck.

"Uh, Lauren. You don't have to get quite so close."

"What? Oh, sorry. Just curious to see the kind of mail a real CPA gets every day."

The resentment in Lauren's voice sent a chill down Ashley's spine. She leaned away, wanting to put even more distance between them.

"Sorry," Lauren said, sounding contrite. "I know all of this is my fault. I was jealous of your success, and desperate. Please forgive me." Her eyes filled with tears.

Ashley gave her friend a quick hug. "Stop apologizing. Let's just make it through the next few minutes and hopefully help will arrive soon. Dillon's an amazing man. If anyone can get us out of this mess, he can. We need to be ready to move."

SO FAR DILLON'S plan was working. He'd gathered a small herd of ten horses in addition to Boomerang. And he figured since no one had shot at him yet that no one had seen him. His hope was they'd be too distracted by the group of horses to notice one man lying low against the neck of the lead horse.

He was fifty yards from the barn where Griffin and his men were being held when a man hopped over the fence by the barn. He cupped a match against the slight breeze and lit the cigarette dangling between his lips as he strode down the length of the barn. He leaned against the wood, took a deep puff from his cigarette. His brows lowered in obvious confusion as he watched the horses trotting toward him. Suddenly his gaze clashed with Dillon's, and held. He dropped the cigarette and clawed for the gun at his hip.

Dillon cursed and slapped the stallion's flank, whipping him into a gallop. The trail horses whinnied and followed his lead. The man dropped to his knees, both hands wrapped around the gun, looking for a clear shot. Dillon aimed the stallion directly at the gunman.

The man's eyes widened and he jerked around, running back toward the fence. Dillon waited until the last second, then threw his leg over the stallion's back and leaped from the horse onto the man, grabbing him around the neck and twisting as they both fell to the ground.

The flash of hooves had Dillon diving out of the way. He rolled under the fence just as the herd dodged to the side, their shrill whinnies filling the air as they whipped back toward the pasture. In their wake, the gunman's body lay broken and lifeless, facedown in the dirt.

One down, but how many more to go?

Dillon slid under the fence, pocketed the man's gun and crept toward the back of the barn.

ICEMAN FLATTENED HIS palms against the tabletop and leaned down, his fierce gaze narrowing at Ashley. "How much longer?"

Her hands froze on the keyboard and her mind raced, trying to think of another excuse, anything to buy some time.

"I think we're close," Lauren said beside her. "Give us a few more minutes."

His gaze shot to Lauren's and he abruptly nodded and went back to the doorway, where he lounged against the doorframe talking to the other gunman.

"Thanks," Ashley whispered. "My mind went blank. I didn't know what to say."

"Open that email, right there. It's from David." The excitement on Lauren's face confused Ashley even more than her words.

"What are you talking about? *Your* David? David Dunlop? Why would he send me an email?"

"Just open it already." Lauren reached over and clicked the email. A slow smile spread across her face. "This is it!" She tugged the laptop toward her. "Luther, you were right. David sent the account numbers to Ashley. We've got it!"

Bile rose in Ashley's throat as she stared in horror at Lauren.

Iceman hurried to the table and read the email over Lauren's shoulder. He smiled, and then he kissed her.

Ashley clutched her hand against her chest as Lauren's triumphant gaze locked on hers.

"Fooled you, didn't I?" she gloated. "Do you know how much I hated being in the back of that van with you, having to pretend to be your friend? But I did it. I bided my time, hoping my theory was right, that David had contacted you somehow to give you the account information. And I was right." She looked up at Luther, her obvious infatuation for him shining in her eyes. "I was right, wasn't I?"

"Yes, you certainly were."

"I don't—I don't understand," Ashley whispered.

"Not as smart as people think you are, are you, *Ash?*" Lauren laughed. "Luther and I used David as our pawn, to get to the money. But he saw Luther and me together at a stupid restaurant, of all places. We were so careful, and the one time we slipped up, David saw us. When I got home, he confronted me, told me he was going to expose me for the fraud I was and tell everyone what I'd done, starting with you."

Her eyes fairly blazed with the hatred Ashley had never known existed.

"Unfortunately, he was far more clever than I thought.

He moved the money out of the account right before Luther killed him. We didn't realize David had double-crossed us until we went to get our money and it was gone."

While she spoke, bitterness dripping from every word, Luther sat beside her and typed on the laptop.

Lauren cupped her chin in her palm. "It was my theory that David had somehow sent you the information. Luther wanted to hold you hostage and torture the information out of you. But I knew what a goody-two-shoes you are. I told him if you knew you had the information, you'd have gone to the police. So it was my idea to make you think I was a hostage, too, so I could trick you into finding the account information for us. For once," she spat out, "I was the smart one. I was more clever than you!"

"I thought we were friends," Ashley said, the words barely above a whisper as she forced them past the cold lump of fear in her throat.

"Friends?" she sneered. "How could I be friends with someone who always thought they were better than me?"

Luther finished typing and closed the laptop. He stood and motioned to the other man at the doorway.

"But I never thought—" Ashley started to say.

"Shut up. Shut up!" Lauren shoved her bangs out of her face. "You don't get to talk to me anymore. Me and Luther are going to—"

Luther grabbed Lauren's arm and pulled her up out of her chair.

"Honey, stop," she said. "You're hurting me."

He shoved her toward Ashley's side of the table and drew his gun. "Get over by her."

The other man stopped beside him and pointed his gun at them, too.

Lauren's face wrinkled with confusion. "What are you doing? We got the money. I don't need to pretend to be her friend anymore."

"Oh, Lauren," Ashley said. "Don't you see it? He used you, too, like you used me."

Lauren shook her head. "No, no! He didn't. He loves me. Luther, you love me." She stared at him, her confusion turning to dismay. "Don't you?" she whispered, sounding like a lost little girl.

He ignored her, turning to the man beside him. "The money is in my account now. Go get the others. I'll finish this."

The man nodded and hurried from the room.

Luther pointed his gun at Lauren.

"Wait, wait!" She jumped up from her chair and ran to the corner of the room. "Luther, look! I can still help you. That detective you thought you'd killed is still alive." She whipped the chair away from the monitor. Luther crossed the room to stand beside her.

How could you, Lauren? Ashley thought, even as she took advantage of their distraction and hurried across the room to the door. She paused, unable to resist a quick glance at the monitor, as well.

In the middle of the screen, right beside the barn, a body lay in the dirt. But he was too small, his hair too light to be Dillon. Relief flashed through Ashley.

Luther leaned in close to study the monitor.

Ashley dashed from the room. She raced to the end of the hallway under the stairs.

"Luther, no, don't!" Lauren's cry sounded behind her.

Ashley whirled around, expecting to see Luther pointing a gun at her, but he wasn't there.

Bam! A gunshot echoed from the library. *Oh, no, Lauren.* Grief and regret slammed into Ashley, making her double over. Luther appeared in the library doorway. He raised his gun. Ashley jerked back and ran around the corner. *Bam!* Wood exploded next to her head, raining splinters and sawdust down on her. She cried out and sprinted for the front door.

THE KNIFE SLASHED down, narrowly missing Dillon's shoulder. He slammed his fist into the other man's jaw and sent him spinning across the barn. The knife went flying and embedded itself in one of the stall doors. Dillon dove for one of his guns that the other man had made him toss when he got the drop on him. The other man saw his intent and dove, as well. They both grabbed the gun at the same time and grappled for control, rolling across the floor.

"Jack, Jack! Help!" the man yelled.

Dillon cursed. There must be another gunman close by. He twisted his body, lying half on top of the other man, but he still couldn't get control of the gun. Footsteps pounded against the dirt outside, coming closer, closer.

In desperation, Dillon lunged forward and bit the other man's wrist.

The man screamed in agony and let go of the gun.

Dillon slammed the man's head against the floor. His eyes rolled up and his body went limp. The footsteps were close, too close. Dillon twisted his body around and aimed the gun two-handed at the door just as another stranger stepped into the doorway, pointing his gun at Dillon.

The man suddenly stiffened and slowly raised his hands.

Chris stepped into the opening, his pistol pointed at the man's head. The white *SWAT* letters seemed to glow against his black flak jacket in the dimness of the barn's interior.

"The cavalry's here," he announced. He grinned as the other four SWAT team members hurried into the barn.

"It's about time." Dillon shoved himself off the floor. "Some Billy the Kid you are."

"I don't see you doing much better, John Wayne. How many more bad guys?"

"Iceman's still unaccounted for. I got one outside the barn, plus this guy. He was calling for Jack, asking for help." He waved toward the man Max was holding and Donna was currently handcuffing. "If that guy isn't Jack, there's another one close by, within earshot."

Chris pointed at two of the team members. "Check it out."

They nodded and headed out the back door again.

"That's the tack room." Dillon pointed to the door with the wood propped in front of it. "Griffin and the farmhands should be in there."

Chris kicked the boards out of the way while Dillon checked his gun's loading and grabbed another gun off the floor.

The farm hands spilled out of the room, their wide-eyed faces mirroring their relief. On the floor behind them, Griffin clutched his hurt leg but waved his other hand, letting Dillon know he was okay.

Bam! Bam! Bam!

Dillon twisted around. He looked toward the house, where the gunshots had come from.

"We've got this," Donna yelled.

Max shoved their prisoner into the tack room and squatted down beside Griffin. He motioned back to Dillon. "Go, go!"

Dillon and Chris ran out of the barn and sprinted toward the house.

"You go in the back," Dillon yelled. "I've got the front."

Chris signaled that he'd heard him and ran to the back porch. Dillon was halfway up the front steps when he heard an engine revving. He whirled around. A man stood in the rear passenger door opening of the green sedan parked behind the white van. He raised his gun. Dillon fired. The man whirled around and fell into the dirt.

The car's tires spun and it took off. Dillon caught a glimpse of Ashley's long hair in the front passenger seat just before the car topped the hill and disappeared.

He swore and leaped off the steps, landing in a crouch. He tore off back toward the barn.

The sound of someone running behind him had him twisting around, pointing his gun.

"It's me," Chris yelled, sprinting to catch up with him.

Dillon didn't stop. He doubled his efforts to reach the barn.

"What are you doing?" Chris demanded, sounding far away as he tried to catch Dillon.

Dillon fairly flew through the barn, digging his keys out as he ran past a startled-looking Donna and Max. He veered right and hopped the fence between the barn and the shed. His Jeep was fifty yards away. His long strides ate up the distance and he hopped into the front seat. He started the engine just as Chris ran out of the barn.

"Dillon! Wait!"

"Can't! Iceman has Ashley!" Dillon floored the accelerator and took off, praying he'd reach the highway before the sedan disappeared.

ICEMAN BARELY SLOWED the car for the sharp left turn at the end of the road from Dillon's farm. Tires screeched and the car banked hard, almost bottoming out before straightening and tearing off down the rural highway.

He steered with his left hand and kept his pistol pointed at her with his right.

She bit her lip, debating whether to try to grab the gun.

His gaze slid toward her. "The only reason you're alive is because Jack called and warned me the SWAT team had arrived. You're my insurance if I need a hostage. But if you give me any trouble, I can always get another hostage. You're completely expendable. Got that?"

She nodded and slid closer to the door so he wouldn't think she was going to try anything. What *could* she try, other than trying to grab his gun? She had no weapons, no phone, no way to fight him or escape. The grass beside the road went by so fast it was a blur. She could always jump. But at this speed, the fall would kill her. Was there some way to make him slow down? How slow would he have to drive for her to survive jumping from the car?

ONCE AGAIN, ICEMAN had Ashley in a car and was too far ahead for Dillon to catch up. He ground his teeth in frustration, wishing he had a faster car. The green sedan topped the next hill and disappeared.

Dillon's accelerator was already to the floor. He fished out his cell phone and called Chris. "He's heading east on County Road 224. I need air support and roadblocks."

"You're a fool, Dillon. You should have waited for me!"

"If I'd waited I wouldn't have even known what

direction he went. Call the state police and get a chopper in the air before he disappears." He hung up without waiting for Chris's response.

He topped the next hill, relieved to see he was gaining on the sedan. But he wasn't gaining on him nearly fast enough. There were a lot of turns coming up, and then the intersection with the interstate. If Iceman reached the interstate before Dillon caught up to him, and before the state police could offer air support, he could blend in with traffic or pull off an exit ramp and hijack another vehicle before anyone knew what was happening.

He slammed his fist against the steering wheel. He had to do something. Now. He had to find a way to get ahead of Iceman and stop him before he reached the interstate.

Praying he wasn't making a horrible mistake that would cost Ashley her life, he slowed the Jeep, then barreled into one of the many cornfields that bordered County Road 224.

THE CAR TOPPED the next hill. A bright red Jeep sat at the bottom of the hill, parked sideways, with a massive flat trailer full of hay bales hooked behind it, completely blocking the road from shoulder to shoulder.

Iceman swore and slammed the brakes. The car fishtailed sideways and came to a bouncing stop. Ashley shoved the door open and dove out of the car. Deafening shots echoed through the air, too many for her to count. She covered her ears and lay half under the car, curled up in a fetal position.

And then the noise stopped.

She lay there, afraid to even breathe. Her heart pounded so loudly in her ears that for a moment she thought someone was shooting again. She should run.

She knew she should run. But she couldn't get her legs to move, and she couldn't seem to force her hands down from over her ears.

Gravel crunched on the shoulder of the road. She squeezed her eyes shut.

"Ashley? Honey, it's me. Dillon. It's over. You're safe. Ashley?"

She slowly opened her eyes, afraid to hope. But there he was, crouching down beside her, his gray-blue eyes looking at her with concern. He wasn't bleeding. He wasn't dead.

Thank you, Lord. Thank you, thank you, thank you. Dillon is safe.

And suddenly, it was all too much. Horrible images flooded through her mind. Stanley Gibson, crumpling to the floor. The truck, plunging into the cold, raging river. Lauren's terrified voice crying out, moments before that first, horrifying gunshot from the library. She covered her face with her hands and started sobbing, her shoulders shaking so hard they scraped across the rough asphalt.

And just as suddenly, she was in Dillon's lap. His strong arms held her tightly against him. His hand rubbed up and down her back and he whispered soothing, nonsensical words in her ear. She put her arms around his neck and sat there in the middle of the highway, crying for all the people who'd been hurt, all the lives that had been destroyed, all because she'd been too busy, too self-absorbed, to see the pain buried deep inside the woman she'd once considered her best friend in the whole world.

Chapter Sixteen

Yesterday, after having a major meltdown on the highway in Dillon's arms, Ashley had been too exhausted and drained to give her statement to the police. Dillon had dropped her off at her rental house after making her promise to come to the station in the morning to wrap everything up.

A full night's sleep and a hot shower had worked wonders. And now Ashley was sitting in the Destiny Police Department squad room across the desk from Dillon, writing up her final statement.

A thud sounded behind Ashley, making her jump. She turned in her chair to see Patricia Dunlop standing in the open front door to the police station. The woman's eyes narrowed when she saw Ashley, and she marched toward her.

"I want that woman arrested," Mrs. Dunlop sneered.

Suddenly Dillon was standing in front of Ashley's chair, blocking the other woman from reaching her. Chris and Max hurried over from their desks and flanked him. The chief must have heard the commotion, as well, because he hurried out of his office and disappeared behind the male wall surrounding Ashley.

"Mrs. Dunlop," he said. "I already told you on the

phone that the charges against Miss Parrish have been dropped. The FBI and the Destiny Police Department are satisfied that she had no involvement with embezzlement or illegal activity of any kind."

"I don't believe that for one second," the woman insisted in a snide voice, making Ashley shudder at the hate that leached out from every word. "I want my money, and I know she knows where it is."

"Your husband's company's money was wired to an offshore account by Mr. Luther Kennedy. As I previously explained, the FBI is actively working to try to get the money returned, but it will take time. And until the court settles the dispute over your husband's will, even if we had the money we couldn't give it to you."

"This is an outrage," she complained. "How am I supposed to live? I need that money."

"Again, as I already explained on the phone," the chief said, sounding far more patient than Ashley could have been in his position, "you can petition the courts to increase your stipend. If they agree the need is there, they'll provide an increase from the estate."

"Let me talk to that woman! All I need is two minutes and I can get the account information from her."

Feet shuffled from behind the wall of protection, followed by an outraged shriek.

"Get your hands off me this instant!"

"I'm happy to talk to you and reexplain everything," the chief assured her. "But only if you quit trying to speak to Miss Parrish and come sit in my office."

"I'll do no such thing. The only person I'll be speaking to is my lawyer. I assure you, this is *not* over."

The front door banged open again, and the wall of men blocking Ashley's view visibly relaxed. Dillon went back to his seat across from her. Chris and Max both gave Ashley reassuring smiles before taking their seats at their desks in the next aisle. And the chief headed to the kitchenette and started making himself a cup of coffee.

"Well, that was…exciting." Ashley gave a nervous laugh.

"If she calls you or harasses you in any way, let me know." Dillon signed her statement and turned it around for her to sign.

When she finished, she put the pen down and blew out a relieved breath. "It feels good to be done with this. It still doesn't feel real that it's all over."

He nodded and shoved the statement into a folder. "I suppose you're going back to Nashville now. Your contract is finished and you have to get back to work."

She frowned, wondering why he was acting so formal. "Yes, my contract is finished. And I do have to get out of the rental today. My landlord already has a long-term lease with the new tenants, and they're anxious to move in."

"Sounds good. Your car's in good working order? No problems?"

"Uh, no. No problems. I drove it here."

"Good. Don't forget to change the batteries in that key fob. You're going straight to Nashville?"

She didn't answer. She waited until he finally looked at her.

"Actually, I'm going back to my hometown first, Sweetwater. The coroner released Lauren's body this morning and her parents are flying her home. I want to be there for the funeral."

He nodded, his gaze sliding away from hers.

She fisted her hands in her lap. "After that," she continued, "I guess I'm going back to Nashville." She hesitated. "Unless…I mean, well, I could come back here…if there was a reason. That is, if you…needed me to?" She waited, hoping, watching him.

He cleared his throat and tucked the folder into his top drawer before crossing his arms on top of his desk. "No. I think we've got everything we need. The FBI has cleared you of all charges, in spite of what Mrs. Dunlop said. Their investigation will continue until every little detail is covered, but as far as this office is concerned, the case is closed." His gaze finally met hers again. "There's no reason for you to come back. But thank you for offering, just the same."

His words hit her like a blow, making her spine stiffen in her chair. She blinked and looked around. Chris was one desk away, his jaw hanging open. Max had his arms crossed and was glaring at Dillon. Even the chief was staring at them, his coffee suspended midair as if he was about to take a drink and had stopped when he heard Dillon's words.

Ashley's face heated as she realized everyone in the station had witnessed Dillon's rejection of her. With as much dignity as she could manage, she pushed her chair back and stood.

"Thank you, Detective Gray. I owe you my life, many times over. I'll always be grateful for everything you and your team did to help me." She offered Chris and the others a watery smile, then slowly turned and walked out of the station.

As soon as the front door closed, Dillon raised his gaze and watched Ashley walk down the sidewalk to her car and out of his life. He ached to call her back, to tell her he wanted her to stay. But what did he have to offer her? She'd made it more than clear she hated small towns.

And he couldn't imagine living in a city. But even more than that, he didn't think he could survive if he allowed himself to love her and then lost her. No, it was better not to even go down that road.

Someone shoved him and he jerked around in his chair.

Chris planted his hands on the desk and glared at him. "You, my friend, are a complete moron and a jerk. Did you not realize she was giving you an opening, that she *wanted* you to ask her to stay?"

Dillon turned back to the papers on his desk. "Butt out. It's none of your business."

Chris swore. "You *did* know what she was asking. So why didn't you even try to talk to her? Everyone who's seen you two together knows there have been sparks flying between you since the day you met. What are you so afraid of?"

"I said, it's none of your business. Back off."

"Fine. You don't want her. Maybe she'll be interested in a guy like me. Maybe I'll head over to her house and—"

Dillon shot out of his chair and grabbed Chris by the front of his shirt. "Leave her alone."

"No. She's beautiful and smart and sexy—"

"And out of your league," Dillon growled. "And even if she would agree to date a sorry soul like you, she wouldn't hang around for long and she'd end up breaking your heart so she could go back to the city." He shook Chris. "Or worse, she'll make you fall in love with her and then she'll do something foolish like jump in front of a speeding car to save a dog or something stupid like that. She'll just up and die on you."

Chris's eyes widened. "Is that what you're afraid of? That if you love her she'll end up dying? Dillon, man, she isn't Harmony. You can't live your life afraid to love someone because you think they'll die on you."

Dillon released his shirt and shoved him out of his way. "We're done here." He grabbed his suit jacket off the back of his chair. "I'm taking the day off."

"Hold up." The chief met him halfway to the door with his cell phone in his hand. "The coroner's report on Luther Kennedy said someone stitched up his shoulder, the shoulder Miss Parrish shot on Cooper's Bluff. And I just got a call from Dr. Brookes's office manager. When she arrived at his office this morning, his car was in the parking lot but he wasn't there. And he's not answering his cell phone. Stop by there on your way home and do a wellness check."

Dillon nodded and headed out the door. He hopped into his Jeep and had just started the engine when Chris got in on the passenger side.

"Get out."

"Stuff it. I'm going with you. Deal with it."

Dillon cursed and shoved the Jeep in Reverse, then peeled out of the parking lot. Twenty minutes later he and Chris were in Dr. Brookes's living room, helping him onto the couch. Dillon worked at the duct tape still wrapped around the man's wrists while Chris held a glass of water to his dry, cracked lips.

"An ambulance is on the way. They'll be here in a few minutes," Chris said.

Dillon tossed the duct tape on the coffee table. "From what you've told us, it sounds like Luther Kennedy is the man who abducted you and made you sew up his shoulder. He's dead now. You don't have to worry about him coming back and hurting you again."

Brookes gave him a shaky smile. "Thank you, Detective, both of you. I don't know how much longer I could have lasted on that floor all taped up like that."

Sirens sounded outside, getting closer.

"You said that man is dead? Did you catch his partner?"

"Partner?" Dillon asked.

"The woman he spoke to on the phone. They were arguing about how to find some account, something about getting their money out."

"You heard her? He had her on speaker?"

"No, no. He said her name."

"Lauren?"

Brookes shook his head. "No, Trisha."

Dillon shot a look at Chris.

"Are you sure about that?"

"Positive. Why?"

Dillon took off at a run.

"Wait!" Chris called out behind him.

Dillon raced down the front steps, past two startled-looking EMTs who'd just gotten out of the ambulance. He hopped in the Jeep and wheeled it around, then slammed on his brakes.

Chris stood in the road directly in front of him with his gun drawn.

"If you try to go around me, I swear to God I'll shoot out your tires," Chris yelled.

"What are you doing? You heard the doctor. Patricia Dunlop was Luther's partner. She could be at Ashley's house right now."

"You're right, which is why we need to get over there. But you're *not* doing this alone. One of these days you're going to get killed because you're so busy trying to be the hero. You *have* to learn to trust someone else again. Trust *me*."

Frustration roiled inside Dillon. He clenched his hands on the steering wheel, sweat popping out on his forehead as he pictured Ashley facing yet another person trying to kill her. The last time she'd nearly died. If he hadn't plowed through that cornfield and gotten ahead of Luther's car, she would have died.

No, that wasn't true. Or at least, he couldn't be sure. Chris had called for the air support, and the roadblock would have been in place before Iceman reached the interstate. Dillon hadn't known that at the time, of course, but he'd learned about it later. And back at the barn, if Chris and the SWAT team hadn't showed up when they had, he might not have made it to the house in time to see Ashley being taken by Iceman.

He forced himself to ease his grip on the steering wheel. Maybe Chris was right. Maybe it *was* time he learned to trust someone else for a change.

"Get in. Hurry up."

Chris shoved his gun in his holster and ran to the passenger side. He hopped through the open plastic window into the seat without even opening the door.

"Show-off," Dillon accused.

"Being younger has its perks."

Dillon rolled his eyes and floored the accelerator. "I'm only two days older than you."

"It shows, man. It shows."

"Make yourself useful and find out Ashley's phone number. We need to call and warn her that Cruella de Vil might be stopping in for a visit."

ASHLEY LOOKED AROUND the house one last time. Since the place had come furnished, including a kitchen fully stocked with pots, pans and dishes, all she'd had to pack were her clothes and what few personal items she'd brought—which basically amounted to her laptop.

She hadn't expected to feel nostalgic about leaving, but it seemed that everything had changed since she'd come to live here four, no, almost five, weeks ago. What she'd gone through had changed her, too, and she wasn't sure yet if that was good or bad. The only thing she was sure of was that she'd miss Dillon Gray far more than he deserved after the way he'd coldly dismissed her at the station.

Forgetting him was at the top of her to-do list once she got out of Destiny, Tennessee. But that was hard to do when she had a picture of him in her palm. She looked down at the tiny gold locket she'd just discovered in her jeans pocket, the jeans she'd been wearing when she'd been at Dillon's parents' house.

When Iceman had pulled her out of the house, she'd fought with everything she had, desperate to get away and help Dillon. She remembered her hands flailing for something to hold on to and raking across the mantel. Her fingers had caught something and she'd later shoved it in her pocket and had forgotten about it. She'd grabbed the locket that contained the picture of Dillon and his family.

She'd have to give it to him, of course. Maybe it would help take the sting out of the horrible loss he and his parents would suffer after losing all those personal mementos in the fire. But she sure wasn't giving it to him in person. She'd mail it to him when she got back to Nashville.

After gently closing the locket, she slid it into her pants pocket, grabbed her purse and headed out the door. Her car was already packed, and there was nothing else to do. It was time to go.

She'd just reached her car when another car pulled down the long gravel driveway, coming toward her. She shaded her eyes against the sun, but she couldn't make out who was behind the windshield. Was the new tenant already here? Leaning against her car, she waited until the other car pulled to a stop behind hers.

Farther down the driveway, a familiar red Jeep turned down the drive. Dillon? What was he doing here? And why was he driving so fast?

A prickle of unease slid down her spine. The driver's door opened on the car behind hers and Patricia Dunlop stepped out with a gun in her hand.

Ashley pivoted to run.

"Don't move!"

She stiffened, cursing herself for not running as soon as the car turned down the driveway. The way her life had gone lately, she should have assumed the car would be carrying another person bent on killing her.

Mrs. Dunlop grabbed her and shoved Ashley in front of her like a shield as the Jeep jerked to a stop beside Dunlop's car. But it wasn't Dillon sitting in the driver's seat. It was Chris Downing.

"Don't come any closer," the woman ordered, as she shoved her gun against Ashley's spine, "or I'll kill her."

Chris slowly opened the door. "I'm just getting out of the car. I want to talk. I won't come any closer."

Dunlop turned the gun and pointed it at Chris. "I don't want to talk. I'm taking this woman with me and we're going to get my money. Close your door and get out of here right now."

"Oh, I don't think that's going to happen."

Bam!

Chris fell to the ground.

Ashley gasped in horror.

The gun fired again, but this time straight up in the air as Dillon wrenched it out of Mrs. Dunlop's hand. Somehow he'd managed to sneak up behind them. He shoved the gun in his waistband at the small of his back and quickly handcuffed Mrs. Dunlop.

Chris rolled over and slowly staggered to his feet, rubbing his chest. "Son of a… You couldn't grab her a second sooner?"

"Oh, quit whining. I got shot three times at Cooper's Bluff."

"Are you okay, Chris?" Ashley called out.

"He's wearing a vest. He's fine."

Chris rubbed his chest. "Speak for yourself. Hurts like the devil."

"Let me go," Mrs. Dunlop yelled. "I demand you let me go. My lawyers are going to—"

"Shut up," Ashley, Dillon and Chris all said at the same time.

Mrs. Dunlop snapped her mouth shut and glared at them.

"Why didn't you answer your phone?" Dillon asked Ashley. "We tried to warn you we found out she was working with Iceman."

"Dead battery."

He shook his head. "You have a problem replacing batteries, don't you?"

"Everyone has their own crosses to bear in life. What happens now?"

"We take her back to the station and book her on attempted kidnapping and a host of other charges."

"I didn't kidnap her. I didn't do anything. My lawyer—"

"Shut up," they all said again.

She glared at them and muttered something under her breath.

"Do I have to stay in town now?" Ashley asked.

Dillon looked away. "No. You can give your statement over the phone once you're home and settled in."

Chris shook his head and glared at Dillon worse than Mrs. Dunlop had. He led her to the Jeep and settled her in the back, then handcuffed her to the roll bar.

Ashley sighed and reached into her jeans pocket. She held the locket out to Dillon.

He frowned and took it. "What's this?"

"It was on the mantel at your parents' house. My hand brushed against it when Iceman was pulling me out of the house. I'd forgotten it until I was packing to leave."

She didn't wait for him to open the locket. She got into her car, started the engine, then pulled into the yard, making a wide circle around Mrs. Dunlop's car and the Jeep. When she reached the end of the gravel driveway, she couldn't resist one final look back in her rearview mirror.

Dillon stood in the middle of the driveway, a good distance away from the cars, as if he might have run after her. But as she watched and waited, he turned away and headed back toward the Jeep, in no apparent hurry. If he *had* chased her, he'd obviously changed his mind.

She made it all the way to the interstate before she burst into tears.

Chapter Seventeen

Another long day of work, another day when Ashley wanted to do anything but step out of her home office and face the rest of her empty apartment. Which was why she was once again sitting on a bar stool, nursing a bottle of beer, staring into the mirror above the bar and wondering how she'd become the pathetic woman who was on a first-name basis with the bartender.

No, she didn't really wonder. She knew the answer. Nearly two weeks ago she'd experienced the most terrifying, horrible and strangely wonderful days of her life. She'd suffered deep loss and numbing fear, and yet had somehow come out of the experience with an understanding of what really mattered, and a glimpse of a future that could have been…magical—if only Dillon hadn't been too stubborn to recognize what he had right in front of him.

She tilted her bottle to her lips, then froze. In the mirror above the bar, familiar blue-gray eyes she never thought she'd see again locked onto her. Standing right behind her, looking taller than she remembered and sexier than any man had a right to look in a white button-up shirt tucked into blue jeans, was Dillon Gray.

His gaze slid away from hers. He sat on the bar

stool beside her and ordered a bottle of beer from the bartender.

Ashley slowly set her bottle down and waited, watching him in the mirror. Her hungry gaze caressed every inch of those broad shoulders, those powerful arms that had protected her and then held her so sweetly, and the barely there stubble that made her fingers itch to touch him.

When his drink arrived, he took a long, slow pull, then set it down. He studied the polished wood surface in front of him as if it held all the secrets of the world. "Thank you for the locket. It means the world to my parents, and to me." His deep voice stroked across Ashley's nerve endings like the richest silk.

"You're welcome," she whispered, still in shock that he was even there.

His fingers idly drew tiny circles on the bar. "I suppose I could get used to a city. I could even live in a city, I suppose, if I had to. I hear they have horses in Nashville. It could work." He took another deep sip of his beer.

Ashley took a drink, too, before she trusted her voice to respond. "I suppose I could get used to a small town again. After all, I spent most of my life in one. I've even heard *some* small towns are so advanced they actually have access to the internet, which would be really handy since I work from home sometimes." She shrugged. "I could live there, I suppose, if I had to. It could work."

His lips curved in a tiny smile that quickly faded. He reached into his shirt pocket and set something on the counter.

Ashley blinked at the tiny silver disc. "What is that?"

"A battery. For your key fob. I looked up your type of car on the internet to make sure I got the right one."

Her throat tightened. "Thank you," she whispered.

He nodded. "I've been told I have trust issues. I never got it before, but I've done a lot of thinking over the past thirteen days, ten hours and—" he looked at his watch "—twenty-three minutes. I realize now that sometimes I have to let others take the lead. And that I can't really *live* if I don't let others in, if I don't share both the good and the bad with the people who matter most." His gaze collided with hers in the mirror. "You matter, Ashley. You matter very, very much."

Tears gathered in her eyes.

"Harmony was my baby sister," he said, so quietly she almost didn't hear him. "She died when I was at college. She was never a good swimmer, but she dove into a pool to save a friend instead of running to get someone else who was a better swimmer. They both drowned." He closed his eyes briefly, as if in pain, then opened them again and recaptured her gaze. "I suppose I've always blamed myself for not teaching her to be a better swimmer. And I've always been…terrified…that someone would die on my watch someday, because I allowed the person who wasn't as experienced or as good as me to jump in and take the lead. Like I said, it all comes down to trust. But I'm trying. I'm really trying."

As he watched her in the mirror, he slowly slid his hand across the bar, palm up.

Ashley met him halfway and placed her hand in his. His fingers closed over hers, his gentle touch warming her all the way to her heart.

"Tell me about Harmony," she whispered. "What was she like?"

His breath left him in a shaky rush, and for a moment she thought she'd pushed too far. But then his fingers gently squeezed hers.

"She was six years younger than me," he began, haltingly at first. But as he continued to speak and share his memories of his beloved sister, his voice grew stronger and his smile widened. And for the first time since Ashley had met him, his smile finally reached his eyes.

The future didn't worry her anymore. She didn't care if she lived in a big city or a small town, because she'd finally discovered that home wasn't about where you lived. It was about who you loved. And when she'd met Dillon Gray in a little town called Destiny, Tennessee, she'd finally found *her* destiny. How could she doubt that? After all, the man had given her what she needed most. She grinned and picked up the silver disc from the bar.

He'd given her a battery.

* * * * *

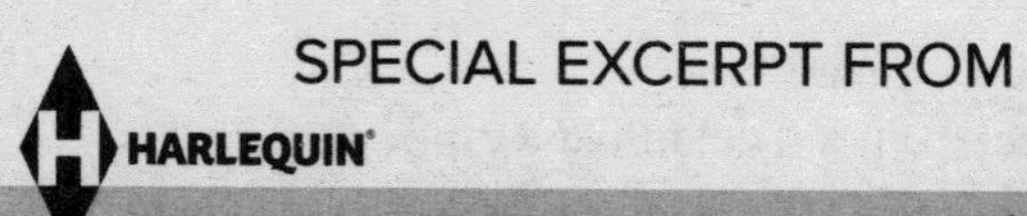

THE SECRET OF CHEROKEE COVE
by Paula Graves

Dana Massey's life is turned upside down, by both a family secret and the offer of protection by the very sexy detective Walter Nix.

"What do you know about the Cumberlands?"

His back stiffened for a second at the sound of the name, and he shot Dana a quick look.

"Why do you ask?" he said.

"My mother's maiden name was Tallie Cumberland. Ever heard of her?"

Dread ran through him like ice in his blood, freezing him as if he was still that little boy from Cherokee Cove who believed every tale his mama told him, especially the scary ones.

"You *have* heard of her."

"I've heard of the Cumberlands."

"Doyle says the most anyone would tell him is that the Cumberlands are nothing but trouble."

"Does that sound anything like your mother?" he asked carefully.

"No."

"Then I wouldn't worry about it."

Dana didn't say anything else until they reached the Bitterwood city limits. Even then, she merely said she'd told Doyle she was going to stay at his house.

"Are you sure you feel safe there?"

"I'm armed, and I'm too wired to sleep."

HIEXP69746

"I could stick around."

"And protect the poor, defenseless girl?"

"Not what I said."

"I'm usually not this prickly. It's been an unsettling night."

"I'm serious about sticking around. Couldn't hurt to have an extra set of ears to listen out for danger."

"And it wouldn't hurt to have some extra firepower," she admitted. "But it's a lot to ask."

"You didn't ask. I offered."

"So you did." Her lips curved in a smile that softened her features, making her look far more approachable than she had for most of the drive.

Far more dangerous, too, he reminded himself.

"I do appreciate the offer to stay, but—"

"But you're a deputy U.S. marshal with a big gun?"

She patted her purse. "Glock 226."

"Nice." He bent a little closer to her, lowering his voice. "I have a sweet Colt 1991 .45 caliber with a rosewood stock, and if you quit trying to get rid of me, I might let you hold it."

A dangerous look glittered in her eyes. "You're trying to tempt me with an offer to handle your weapon?"

He nearly swallowed his tongue.

She smiled the smile of a woman who knew she'd scored a direct hit. "You can stay," she said almost regally. "We'll negotiate weapon-handling terms later."

Will Nix's protection be enough to keep Dana safe?
Find out in award-winning author Paula Graves's
THE SECRET OF CHEROKEE COVE,
on sale March 2014 wherever
Harlequin® Intrigue® books are sold!

HIEXP69746